A Senseless Death in a Dying Republic is John Rook's first novel. In a career spanning 40 years, John has worked as a photographer, teacher and journalist. Apart from photography qualifications, he has a Bachelor of Arts (major: Journalism) and a Masters in Adult Education. He served for 9 years in the Royal Australian Navy as a navy cameraman. John has long been an avid reader of ancient history and studied Ancient History at Macquarie and New England Universities. He is married and lives with his wife at Buff Point in NSW, Australia.

To my wife, Marilyn, my unofficial Editor-in-Residence, and the other ladies in my life:

Kitty, Pauline, Lynn, Anne and Jacqui with gratitude and love.

And to, my father, Johnny, who first opened my eyes to classical literature.

And also to, my son, Eliot, a master of the Freudian world. With love.

John Rook

A Senseless Death in a Dying Republic

Austin Macauley Publishers™
London • Cambridge • New York • Sharjah

This is a work of fiction. Names, characters, businesses, places, events, locales, and incidents are either the products of the author's imagination or used in a fictitious manner. Any resemblance to actual persons, living or dead, or actual events is purely coincidental.

A CIP catalogue record for this title is available from the British Library.

ISBN 9781398414037 (Paperback)
ISBN 9781398414044 (Hardback)
ISBN 9781398414051 (ePub e-book)

www.austinmacauley.com

First Published 2022
Austin Macauley Publishers Ltd®
1 Canada Square
Canary Wharf
London
E14 5AA

Foreword

86 BCE

In 86 BCE, the biggest and proudest metropolis in the known world is Rome. The old cities of Athens, Alexandria, Babylon and Carthage are mere shadows of what they once were. Carthage, for example, is no more, a mere rubble heap, destroyed by Romans after three separate conflicts. And, not for the first time in her history, the city of Rome is in trouble; both with her Latin allies throughout Italy, and with her republican leadership, both Senate and populous.

An unlikely pair of military heroes is at war with each other over their ideas on how the burgeoning city and population should be politically administered, especially during the crisis of civil war with her Italian allies. Men of vision for uniting Italy and extending citizenship, such as Marcus Fulvius Flaccus, Gains Gracchus and Marcus Livius Drusus *have* all died for their efforts to introduce a fairer system of universal Roman citizenship.

Gaius Marius and Lucius Cornelia Sulla are the two mighty men of Rome. Although the pair served many years in the Roman Army and had many military successes, they despised each other. Each had the support of soldiers and the

Roman and Latin citizenry. However, politically, they were poles apart: Gains Marius is a supporter of the *Populares* faction which represented the lower classes of Rome, the plebs—they even had a tribune of the Plebians and the tribune could veto the excesses of the privileged, dominant senators. Sulla, on the other hand, is a supporter of the *Opimates,* the Aristocrats, the Conservatives, descendants of the founding families, who wished to curb the power of the lower classes in the Republic. So now, we have the right ingredients for civil war.

However, Sulla is dispatched to Pontus (Asia Minor) with a large army to curb the expansionist policies of Mithridates, King of Pontus. While Sulla is absent, Marius invades Rome and slaughters many of the Sullan supporters. It is only through the efforts of Lucius Cornelius Cinna that the Marian slaughter is curbed, and Rome returns to relative peace. Meanwhile, Sulla, having dealt with Mithridates via a peace treaty, is on his way back to Rome to deal with Marius and the lower classes.

Their enmity began in the war against Jugurtha, almost forty years before. Sulla was Marius's second in command. Using his own initiative, Sulla, through his own conniving, managed to capture Jugurtha, but Marius, as senior commanding officer, took all the glory for the capture and ultimate defeat of the Jugurthine menace.

Chapter 1

Justinian is just fifteen years of age, and this is the background he has been born into. He is a tall young male and will certainly follow in his father's footsteps and join the military. The prospect of being a soldier for twenty-five years is worrying. He hasn't seen his father for two years, who is in further Spain with the general, Metellus, warring against the rebel Centurion *(pilus prior),* Quintus Sertorious. So far, Sertorious and his bedraggled army of Iberian and Lusitanian mercenaries in Spain have outwitted and proved costly to the Roman legions for eight years. So, Justinian, gloomily, accepts that his father will not be returning to Rome anytime soon.

Justinian also accepts the fact that he now fulfils the role of *pater-familias,* since he is the eldest son. His two sisters, Julia and Antonia, both younger than he, are only now beginning to show him some respect for his newly acquired role in the family hierarchy. It has never been explained to him exactly what this new role is. His mother, Attia, although a fiercely independent woman, acknowledges that this is the way domestic life in a Roman family behaves in accordance with dignitas and tradition. However, mater has managed the running of family, and their slaves, quite satisfactorily for the last few years.

Dignitas, Justinian has difficulty with this term for it is a construct of ideals, passed down from the founding fathers, representing the Roman way, a concept of virtuous and honourable behaviour which binds Rome to herself. It binds Roman people by placing a code of existence for both men and women in areas of bravery, courage and filial responsibility. *Dignitas* separates Romans from barbarians. If you do not possess dignitas, then you are worthless to Rome, lacking virtue and fidelity.

As Justinian dwells on these thoughts once more, his body shudders at the enormity of his newly inherited responsibility to his family and society. At fifteen, Justinian has completed his formal tutelage and he knows that his next obligation is military training. For Justinian, whose ancestry is Cornelian and it belongs to the ancient Roman class of knights, and therefore, he must pursue the *cursus-honorum*, his ladder to success in public life, his civic duty, his course of honour or succession of increasing importance. But he also understands that his is not an aristocratic family, he must work harder for this importance.

This ladder of success in Roman society commences with military service, and then advancement to the Senate, Rome's republican political-law institution. He will have to start at the bottom, *Aedile*, and make his way to the top, the *consulship*, the overall political and military leader of the Roman world. At this stage, he can conquer new territories, wage war and make decisions about Rome's future. However, this must be carried out in conjunction with a fellow consul and the Senate, for the consulship is always a pair of men, one Military, and the other Civic and Law; one to counter-balance the other. Justinian has a long way to go to fulfil his obligations to Rome.

He is confused about things happening in Rome at the moment. Two of Rome's mighty heroes, Marius and Sulla, are in a pitched battle against each other to secure the consulship solely for themselves. Both appointed consuls, but Sulla had been sent overseas to defeat Mithridate's, king of Pontus, a self-appointed ruler of the East, who had waged a murderous vendetta against the Roman people and their servants in the east. Having made peace with Mithridates through diplomatic measures, Sulla, victorious, is on his way back to Rome to reclaim his legally appointed consulship and dispose of Marius once and for all, who had usurped the Senate and unconstitutionally declared himself as sole consul. People in Rome considered Marius had gone insane. Elderly and infirm, Marius, after an illustrious career as Rome's most outstanding general, he had reaped vengeance on those citizens and senators who had besmirched his name and hampered his career in recent years. Justinian shuddered, thinking about the bloodbath that is Rome. Where had dignitas and loyalty to Rome gone these days?

Justinian's thoughts were interrupted by his mother's summons from somewhere in their home. 'Justinian, where are you? I need to talk to you, Justinian…'

'I'm coming, mother' he quickly replied, noting the seriousness in his mother's voice. He shuffled off his bunk, wiping away the crumbs from the front of his tunic and quickly joined his mother.

'Yes, mother, what is it?'

His mother, suddenly short of breath from the rush, managed, 'A letter from Cassius has just arrived, it's news for you.'

Justinian stood up straighter; 'it's an important event, a letter from a senior senator.'

'Let me see it, mother, it must be about my recruitment,' he hastily demanded, not thinking about his manners.

His mother noted the authority in his voice but shrugged and handed him the scrolled letter. Justinian quickly opened the scroll and his eyes darted from left to right, then again, 'I'm to report to garrison headquarters on the Campus Martius tomorrow at dawn for induction and further directions,' he said with a slight tremor in his voice. His mother, attempting a smile, added, 'It's what you've been waiting for,' and was abruptly overcome with dread. Justinian saw his mother pale and quickly grasped her shoulders, 'Mother, please, you know I must do this, it's my duty and obligation to the State. Oh think, mother, I'll be a cadet in the Roman army, attached to some legion, sent to a trouble spot, like father,' he quickly explained, without heeding her state of mind. She was anxious, tears starting to well-up in her eyes, but she understood her son's aspirations. His manhood is quickly overcoming him. He overlooked her tears but hugged her to his body. The pair remained in embrace for some moments, and then Justinian moved to free himself and offered, 'Mother, you must be happy for me because at last I'll be considered important as a Roman soldier. You will be safe here with Alexander, Munius and Edina. They are our slaves but are now part of our household and you know how Edina feels about you and my sisters, she would die for you.' His words were soothing, and his mother felt the effects, she kissed him on the forehead, drawing herself away from him. She understood these moments were meant to be, and that her duty was to let him go. She would pray to the household gods tonight and ask for wisdom and understanding. Things had been difficult enough in her household; she hadn't seen her husband for two years, although she had received letters and he was unharmed. He promised to be home by the Saturnalia. Oh, how she wished time moved more quickly.

Attia had married young, as was Roman tradition. She fell in love with Justinius immediately, at the tender age of fourteen. Her husband-to-be was nineteen and came from a well-respected Roman military family. He was serving under Lucullus as a soldier's tribune. His marriage to Attia ushered in a new respectability and Justinius was quickly promoted to *princeps prior*. Initially, he was brought to the attention of the general Pompei Strabo and was soon transferred, and now served in Spain.

Attia considered herself very lucky, as a mother she had managed to retain her body shape and was considered attractive. Her body was long and athletic. She was headstrong, with a proud heritage behind her. She had a lean, attractive face, full lips, and deep brown eyes. Roman men still propositioned her at banquets. Men took dangerous risks, she didn't. Cassius, the senator, had made himself her unofficial chaperone since her husband left for Foreign Service. In his fifties, he was doddery but caring, talkative but intelligent, stooped but strong in body and didn't tolerate any nonsense.

Justinian left his home and headed for the forum, quite a distance to walk but he enjoyed witnessing the leading men of Rome debating about the current civil unrest. Perhaps he would be lucky today and hear speeches by Rome's leaders like Cornelius Cinna, Cato the Younger or, perhaps, old and stooped Marius, the legendary consul and general. It was worthwhile listening to these senators, leaders, for they were determining the future of mighty Rome.

The topic of Sulla and his intentions dominated the speeches; undeclared civil war and bloody vengeance had produced turmoil and a few of the law-makers had perished by the sword. The ugly spectacles of rioting and proscriptions are imminent, and many fled the city. The population had become divided between Sullan and Marian loyalists.

By mid-afternoon, Justinian was ensconced in the public area of the forum. Attia was attending a chatty afternoon with a group of wives after attending cleaning chores at the Temple of Diana. All of the ladies, except Lydia, had husbands in the military and were currently alone, some had been for months, others, for years. Attia was never comfortable with the group because, gossip dispensed with, the subject was concentrating on one man in Rome called Catalina, a noble, rich and a notorious womaniser; it was once believed he had deflowered a young vestal. Women seemed to swoon in his presence, and, this fact alone, seemed to have many in the group displaying dreamy affection. Attia was not one of them. She knew of Catalina and had come to despise him and his reputation. She had concerns for her daughters. They are now of an age when desires shone through their demeanours and, though scatty and youthful, could possibly be drawn to Catalina's circle of evil friendship, and that would be disastrous.

The ladies' gathering continued until late in the afternoon and Attia was the first to notice how dark the sky was becoming. The day had been sticky, so a storm would be entirely possible. After she had made the comment about the daylight, the other women summoned their slaves to escort them to their homes. Attia hadn't been escorted to the function; she didn't need slaves to assist her get around the safer streets of Rome. But, as she thought more about it, it was silly of her to come alone.

Making their way to the front entrance, Attia brushed against Lydia, the respectable wife of Scaurus, a senior senator. 'Attia, my dear, have you nothing to cover yourself? It does look like rain's coming,' she said, taking Lydia's elbow. Attia replied, 'I'm so silly sometimes, I amaze myself,' quickly adding, 'but, yes, I'm here as is, and I shall get soaked going home.' Lydia was a tall, stately woman with chiselled features and a glowing olive complexion, considered by others as past her prime. Attia, studying Lydia's face, considered her an enchanting lady. However, Lydia had a reputation; being so much younger than her husband, and despite her age, she has a vigorous appetite for weak-willed males. It was believed that even Sulla has bedded her. Apparently Scaurus, the old scoundrel, in his early 80s, didn't mind his wife's passionate appetite. He was happy just to have her by his side at important venues. Leaving the household, Lydia's litter, as well as two stout fellows bearing it, pulled-up directly in front of the ladies. It wasn't raining yet, but dark clouds were massing overhead. Attia smiled at Lydia as she sat herself down in her sedan, 'It looks so comfortable,' she began. 'Oh, yes, I wouldn't be without one, I'm surprised you don't own one,' Lydia replied, offering a smirk. Attia quickly trod away, offering a 'bye, bye,' needing to get home as soon as possible.

The streets of Rome were full of commotion. At first, Attia thought it might be the threatening weather. As she briskly made her way home, she could hear people calling out, 'Sulla's not far,' or 'Sulla's about to enter by the Servian Gate,' or 'Sulla's here for revenge.' Attia, becoming scared, pushed herself to pick a quicker route home. 'Oh, goodness, please look after me, whatever gods are listening,' she muttered. She began to see lots of soldiers wandering around, and almost stumbled over someone lying on the roadway. 'Oh my God,' she screamed, and then, noticing the blood pooling under the body, she gagged and suddenly wanted to be sick.

Not far from the forum there was suddenly an outburst of shouting. A small group of men were running for their lives towards the *Subura*. Once among the crowded tenements and narrow laneways of the *Subura*, they could melt into the local population. Justinian, alarmed, stood on the forum steps and stared, wide eyed, at the fleeing group of men. He could distinctly see one particular man because he was much taller than the rest, Gaius Marius. He was being shouted at by another, younger man, probably Marius junior.

Justinian started to worry about his own circumstances, he was not loyal to either Sulla or Marius, but this approach, he understood, would not win him any favours if drunken soldiers arrived, looking for fights. He must think of a quick way to return home. As he descended the steps, suddenly a man's voice was heard over the din of carousing soldiers. 'Justinian, master, please let me escort you…' Justinian now recognised the voice; it was Munius, one of their household slaves. 'Oh, uh, Munius…ye gods, am I glad to see you!' Justinian exclaimed, then quickly added, 'yes, take me home…' But Munius shook his head, 'No, no, master, *Domina* is missing, we must find her,' Munius grabbed his arm and steered him away from the forum steps, 'Mother's missing, how?' He stammered, 'where did she go?' Munius starts crying and blubbered, 'Domina wouldn't let us accompany her. She had a meeting with other wives this afternoon, um, I think Scaurus's wife is one of them, oh dear, dear.'

Justinian grabbed Munius by the shoulders, 'Stop blubbering, Munius, let's visit Scaurus. He wasn't in the Senate today; he must be home.'

The sky was looking gloomier but still no rain. People were shouting and screaming all over the Subura. Soldiers, swords drawn, were chasing people up alleys and into shadowy doorways. One or two bodies lay on the road. Attia steered herself well away from them, covering her mouth with her shawl. She was now sobbing, frightened of what was taking place in Rome's streets. Suddenly, she heard horses from nearby but couldn't tell which direction they were located from. Probably Roman cavalry, she thought. Then suddenly, four horse soldiers appeared, bursting out of an alleyway, heading straight for her. The noise of the hooves on the cobble roads was deafening and as they drew closer, Attia covered her ears and turned her back on the horsemen. Awaiting the impact, Attia screamed but the horsemen pulled back on their mounts only a few yards from her and a voice was heard, 'Woman, who are you?' She turned towards the horsemen and noticed how resplendent the men were in their military garb and helmets. Three men wore silvered breastplates while the fourth man wore a black breastplate emblazoned with many intricate patterns. This man, with a deeply tanned and lined face, spoke to her again with a commanding voice, ‘Have you no tongue, m’lady, what is your name?’ Suddenly, another horseman quickly added, ‘I do think it is Attia, wife of Centurion Justinius, a Cornelia, serving with Metellae in Spain, Sulla.’

‘Well, that’s splendid, but m’lady, Attia, you need to be indoors. Are you trying to get back to your home?’

Attia nodded and answered, ‘Yes, Sulla, I am.’

‘Then Atticus shall escort you home,’ he swung round in the saddle, ‘Look after this lady, Atticus.’

Justinian, after visiting Scaurus the Younger and speaking to his wife, frowned, ‘Well, I don’t know where mother is. Let’s head back home and see if she’s arrived, Munius.’ So, both swung around and headed back home. Walking in Rome for any reason is fraught with danger. Increased numbers of soldiers in groups were carousing and yelling, damning Gaius Marius and his followers. Scuffles were occurring everywhere but so far, Justinian and Munius had avoided any challenges, they simply appeared as a youth and his slave attendant making their way home. Anyone voicing their support for Marius was soundly cudgelled.

Arriving home, Justinian and Munius were surprised to see a horse tied to a tree branch outside their villa. Justinian made his way indoors and found himself confronting a Roman officer. ‘Who are you?’ the officer asked.

‘I am the son of Justinius and Attia, I live here, where’s my mother?’ he replied rather haughtily.

'Your mother is in her room. I escorted her home, and please address me with some respect for a Roman officer,' he answered with disdain.

'Oh, I'm sorry, sir, um. I was worried for her. Munius and I were looking for her,' Justinian offered, apologetically.

'Now that you are home, please look after your mother. I'm returning to my cohort. I bid you good day,' Atticus responded, and made his way out through the doorway.

Justinian quickly made his way to his mother's room. Rising from her couch, she hugged her son, 'I'm so sorry, son, I've been so foolish. Did you see any bodies on the streets? Oh, it's so frightful…' Justinian calmed her with a hug, 'Mother, you must promise me that you'll never go out without escorts, Munius or Alexander, or even I,' he demanded, then kissed her on the forehead, and added, 'It's too dangerous on the streets. It is not a good time for Romans, and I suspect things will get much worse now that Sulla has returned.'

'I met Sulla with three of his officers,' she told him, excitedly, 'It was Sulla who arranged my escort back home with the young cavalry officer. Sulla doesn't seem so bad.'

'You were very lucky, mother, there's a state of civil war between Romans now, and Sulla's looking for Marius and his cronies, people are going to perish.'

Later in the evening, Justinian was packing a few garments into his carry-all, thinking about the day's events, in particular, his visit to Scaurus's villa. Scaurus the Younger wasn't home but Lydia would see him in her chamber, the servant informed him. The servant took him straight there and lightly tapped on the door. Lydia bade "Enter". Remaining outside, the servant eased the door open while gesturing

Justinian to enter. He was shocked when she rose from her couch. Lydia was dressed in a diaphanous long stola, and he couldn't help but stare distractedly at her breasts down over her slight belly to the shadowy bush at the top of her thighs. He nervously cleared his throat and uttered his apology for disturbing her. Lydia, with a wry smile, replied, 'Why, you're Attia's son, you are welcome, please sit here,' and gently guided him over to the couch. He politely stood while Lydia made herself comfortable, then he sat next to her, at her invitation. Justinian, extremely nervous, uttered, 'Thank you, um, Lady Scaurus,' being so close to her he couldn't help but stare at her crotch beneath her stole. He coughed, 'I'm er, searching for my mother, Attia, did she leave the meeting with you?' Lydia felt his anxiety and also a measure of desire, 'Would you like some watered wine?' He shook his head, uh, er, no thank you, m'lady,' and then he went on to explain how he'd just met one of his household slaves searching for her; he'd been at the forum for most of the afternoon listening to Marius. She, in turn, related how she had left the meeting with Attia but separated when her litter arrived. Attia looked like she was heading for the *Subura.* Justinian left Scaurus the Younger's household, bewildered by Lady Scaurus's behaviour. He shook his head, gave a short whistle and, resumed his search with Munius.

With his mother and sisters safe within their villa, Justinian retired to his dorm. His packing complete, he bid the slaves goodnight and requested Munius to wake him before dawn, so he could easily get to the *Campus Martius*, near the Tiber River. The rain didn't arrive that afternoon and it was still quite sticky. Justinian lay on his bunk and settled himself for sleep. But thoughts of the meeting with Lydia, and especially the way she was dressed, entered his mind. He considered her a slut for revealing herself in front of a mere youth like she did. However, and not surprisingly, he felt his member stiffen. He moaned, thought about the consequences of him remaining with her and sharing some wine. 'Gods,' he groaned and squeezed his eyelids tightly, attempting to block out the memory.

Next morning, Justinian, weary, set off for the *Campus Martius* for his induction into the Roman army. Calm and a degree of stability had returned to the streets of Rome for the moment, but when he arrived at the *Campus Martius* he was shocked at the crowds of soldiers, tents and equipment of war. Through the night, Sulla's vast army had arrived and set up camp. Many of the soldiers had gone into the city, stationed in lots of the districts to ensure that Sulla controlled the city, and, to seek out Marius or Cornelius Cinna and their followers, thus preventing any retaliation. Marius and his son had fled, avoiding arrest. Many braziers throughout the camp sites were still ablaze, giving off heat, so soldiers milled around the warmest sites. Despite the weather being sticky throughout daylight, it still got very chilly during the night. After making several inquiries, Justinian made his way to the recruiting tent. He was greeted by an old, gruff, pockmarked and scarred centurion named Burros asking for his name. Justinian answered and had his name checked off on a papyrus list. He made him make his mark, then read from memory, the Roman army oath of allegiance. In a matter of several minutes, Justinian had now become a Roman soldier, then he was handed a small brass disk and told to report to the outfitter's tent.

His pack was heavy and he found himself sweating as he made his way to return the disk to the recruitment officer. He believed he'd meet some of his friends of the same age going through the same recruiting routine but with so many soldiers milling around, a horn sounded, interrupting his thoughts; his attention was directed to the central area of the camp. Soldiers were running towards some activity. Justinian knew from his studies that the central area of a Roman camp was reserved for the command tents. Judging by the crowds of soldiers gathering, there must be something important taking place, he reasoned. But Justinian was weighed down carrying his kit and utensils and thought about dumping it.

So far, his induction into the Roman army hadn't included anywhere to live. Those affairs would probably come later when I hand back the disk, he considered. So now, Justinian was torn between going to the command tents *(principia)*, and returning his disk to the induction tent. Soldiers were busy filing past him and muttering curses because he was dawdling along, loaded down with kit. 'Get your arse out of the way, laddie. Quickly, move it!' A soldier bellowed, Justinian side-stepped, attempting to get himself out of the way but lost his footing and fell to the damp ground, his kit spilling too. Cooking utensils, drinking mugs, odd uniform garments, hob-nailed sandals, a basic helmet and assorted bags of grain, rice and hard biscuits scattered around him. Justinian eased himself up onto his backside and sat there while pandemonium went on around him. 'Jupiter!' He yelled to anyone who could hear him.

After a short period, the commotion in the camp started to settle. As Justinian sat there, he could hear a strong voice bellowing at the crowd of soldiers. He couldn't make out what the commander was saying, and he didn't know who it was, although he suspected it was Sulla. As he strained to listen, a voice behind him made him jerk. 'Hello there; let me help you up.' Justinian swung around and found himself facing a young officer. 'Oh, goodness, thank you, um, sir.' He tried to get on his feet. The officer offered him a pull up, Justinian was grateful and, once standing, identified his insignia as that of a prefect. He offered the officer a salute with an extended arm, parallel to the ground. The officer simply nodded. Justinian, brushing his tunic down, mumbled an apology and a thank you. 'Be careful, son, around the camp. Soldiers are liable to stampede at any time. If you hear the horn, duck for cover. My name's Agrippa, prefect, IV legion. See the quartermaster, he'll provide you with a tent number,' he paused, 'things have changed rather uncomfortably, most of these soldiers were known as "Marius's Mules" but now they've labelled themselves as "Sulla's Sons of Whores".' He coughed to cover his embarrassment.

'Thank you again, sir, I shall get these things picked up and report to the quartermaster. Um, Sir, by the way, what was the commander saying to the soldiers?' Justinian queried.

'He was telling them that Marius has fled the city with his son and some of his followers. Sulla is offering several talents to anyone who can produce Marius's head.' Agrippa replied, gloomily. 'I better be off now, get settled and I'll see you again sometime.'

Justinian thought, what a good officer, I hope they're all like Agrippa. He was soon to learn that the majority of officers are not so agreeable.

For the remainder of the day, Justinian spent the time organising his billet. He became the fourth occupant of tent

VII, legion IV, under the command of Gneus, son of Strabo. Once he had secured a bunk, he attended to his issued clothing, which included two tunics, body shawls, a helmet without a crest and two pairs of hob-nailed sandals, a crude round shield and a short wooden sword. There were cooking pots, a tankard, assorted items of food, digging utensils and a 'Y' shaped back brace to enable him to strap on items for long marches. He had not been issued with a leather cuirass, javelin (pilus), sword (gladius), or shield. These would come later as he progressed with his basic training. Justinian considered his issued kit and dress rather dull and uninspiring; though he understood that officers, whether noble or equestrian, usually supplied their own cuirass and helmet crest with legion colours and appropriate insignia. However, these items would come later when he completed basic training. For the moment, he would have to function as a drab trainee soldier with a wooden gladius and wooden shield.

Meeting his fellow tent occupants was the next requirement and to his disappointment, the other three fellows were at least four years older than him. This inevitably meant that he would be the tent lackey. He would end up looking after all the menial chores. But, what could he do? This was the way of things in the Roman Army. Pedianus Fuscus, Lucius Julius, Fulvius Antoninus and Marcus Pius, all introduced themselves to Justinian over the first three days of camp life. And contrary to Justinian's initial opinions, they seemed to be fair fellows. Helpful, Pedianus and Fulvius assisted him to square away his kit and showed him how to arrange his cot and space for the inevitable inspections. During these first days, Justinian absorbed lots of information about finding his way around the camp, and where he should be if the camp should come under attack.

'But how can I defend the camp with a wooden sword?' He asked Marcus,

'You won't be fighting anyone if we are attacked. You, my friend, will be a runner, all the new recruits are runners,' Marcus answered, then went on to describe how the runners guaranteed that the orders from command got to the various units around the camp. 'So, if the horns sound, you should race over to the command area and await instructions.'

The following morning, Justinian awoke to a booming voice outside the tent, 'ALL LEGION VIII CADETS GET INTO SINGLE FILE.' Stunned for some moments, he thought he was dreaming and remained in his bunk. Looking around the tent, the other three bunks were vacant and neatly made up.

'THIS IS THE LAST CALL FOR ALL CADETS, IF YOU DON'T GET INTO SINGLE FILE OUT HERE NOW, YOU WILL GO ON REPORT. HEED MY WORDS!' Once more, the booming voice bellowed.

'Gods!' Justinian cursed, and quickly struggled to get off his cot, then slipped-on a long shawl and a pair of sandals and dashed away through the tent doorway. Outside, a single file of six dishevelled youths, stood at attention facing an aged Centurion whose eyes locked on to Justinian.

'Well, prince of Rome, forgive us for disturbing you, you lazy oaf!' The soldier directed to Justinian and spat at the ground. He added. 'How's Rome going to build an empire with soldiers like you who want to stay in bed?'

'Um, sorry, sir, I slept in,' Justinian knew this was a lame excuse but couldn't offer anything else.

'Just fall-in line with the others, son, and do it quickly,' he replied.

Training in earnest had begun.

During the first two weeks of training in the Roman army. Justinian felled sixteen trees, marched for four days straight, officially saluted fifty-eight times, had fourteen swordfights using wooden swords, tossed a javelin eight times, deployed a wooden shield in mock combat four times and, finally, deployed a shield in the tortoise (*testudo*) manner to protect against arrows three times. And, after two weeks of training, Justinian collapsed of exhaustion in his tent. His tent-mates gathered around his prostrate body and offered reassurances that things would get better. 'Now to a degree,' Fulvius began, 'you are now considered as a useful auxiliary, should we have to defeat some enemy. You should be able to carry-out orders in the height of battle,' Fulvius concluded. Justinian nodded, answered, 'But not with a wooden sword.'

Fulvius playfully punched him on the upper arm, 'Justinian, you should receive your real sword after a month. You seem to be progressing fairly well.'

Justinian groaned, rolled over on his side, 'Oh gods, please let me sleep.'

It was exactly fifty-four days until Justinian was presented with his gladius short sword and after his first armed fight ten days later, in which he showed the utmost care in sword handling that he received his crimson crest for his helmet. Justinian was slowly becoming a junior officer in the Roman army. Now he could display some authority but, he was warned by his fellow tent occupants, he needed to be careful who he started ordering around. If by chance he picked on some twenty-year veteran, he would likely lose some teeth. Justinian heeded this advice and managed to keep all his teeth.

His training lasted ninety days and at last, he was marched to the Command tent with three other trainees. They halted near the main entrance and were told to remain at attention until they were summoned to enter. They waited for a considerable period and remaining at attention was becoming a strenuous effort, but finally a youngish voice bid them enter. They trooped in, halted, then faced a senior officer and presented him with their raised arms as a salute. The senior officer returned the salute, then told the men to stand at ease. 'Junior officers, I am Magnus, second in command to Sulla who is in the Senate at the moment so cannot be with us, though he sends his best wishes to the four of you.' He walked up to face the four and pinned an insignia to each of the leather cuirasses. 'This represents your legion, the four of you are now members of legion IV, which is one of mine, and your posts will be under Centurion Agrippa. For all intents and purposes, Agrippa will be your father for this first initial period in the legion. By the way, have any of you got horses? No, well we'll see what we can do to procure some horses.' He went silent for a few moments, inspecting each one of them, and then gestured to their uniforms, 'They're not the best, these uniforms. I suggest when you get your first leave go to the officer's outfitters in the city and get them to make you a uniform, I'm sure your parents will be able to spare some money.' With that, the four young men were dismissed.

Each of the young officers went off in different directions back to their billets, only to be told that they could have the rest of the afternoon off. They also got permission to go into the city but to keep away from the Marian districts. Justinian decided to go home and show himself off to his mother and sisters. Once Justinian reached his home, he noticed there was an air of foreboding about the villa. His sisters wouldn't leave their room, so he sought out his mother. He knocked on her door and detected her slow shuffle to open it. Justinian's face suddenly became a mask of dread as he looked upon his mother's wasted condition. 'Mother!' he exclaimed, while Attia shuddered at the sight of her son and she burst into tears whilst trying to say something. Justinian took her into his arms and lightly squeezed her, lest he crush her now frail body. 'Mother, what has happened? Why are you so distraught? It's not father, is it? Please tell me,' he demanded.

Attia nodded and between sobs answered, 'Father's dead, oh,' Father's dead and so is Quintus Sertorius. The household was in mourning and Attia was inconsolable, 'We cannot get his body for a proper Roman funeral. Oh, ye gods!' she cried, 'What are we to do? Father died for Rome, fighting Rome's wars and this is how we are treated,' she added, and then slumped down on the couch. Justinian, feeling helpless dropped to her side and took her into his arms. 'I shall make some inquiries when I get back to the camp,' he offered, and then realised his mother was not listening to him. 'Please, mother, listen to me. I have to return to camp before sunset. But tomorrow I will ask about his death and see what I can do about getting father back to Rome.' His mother, sobbing, gave him a peck on the forehead,' 'I heard you, son, and yes, and please do that.'

How the hell am I going to get into the general's quarters without a real officer coming along with us, Justinian thought, when suddenly, his two younger sisters entered the room.

Julia and Antonia looked miserable, haggard, in fact. Like Attia, they'd all been through an ordeal, but Justinian couldn't get over how gaunt the pair looked. Julia was the older of the two, only fourteen, while Antonia was a younger twelve. 'Sisters, what have you been doing to yourselves? The pair of you are so scrawny, you both look like starving slaves,' Justinian angrily demanded. Both sisters, as if on cue, started to cry and convulse. 'Oh goodness, stop the bawling and tell me, what's going on?' he demanded. Julia sunk into the couch and appeared to get control of her emotions. 'Brother, um, ever since you've been away, two visitors call on us regularly, mother thinks they are doing this out of kindness and have true intentions concerning our well-being,' Justinian sat up, 'Who are these visitors?'

'Catalina and Fulvia,' she answered guardedly. Justinian shot up, anger masked his face, 'How in the gods' names did Catalina come to learn about our home circumstance?' Julia blushed, stammered, 'Oh, brother, it's all my fault, I'm sorry, uh, I told him of our circumstances.' Justinian thought he got into a rage but instead, he looked over to Antonia, 'Are you a party to this too?' Julia shook her head, 'No, Antonia just follows my lead; you know that I'm the guilty one and besides, Catalina is wooing me, not Antonia.' Justinian stared at Julia silently for a few moments, then was about to lash out, when Attia appeared through the doorway. 'Children, please, stop bickering and think about how proud you are of your father!'

Justinian only had leave until dusk. There was no such thing as compassionate leave in the Roman army, perhaps for commanders, but not for recruit officers. It was unpleasant discussing arrangements around father's death with mother. All he could do was to speak to his commanding officer,

Lucullus. As for the other business of 'Catalina's relationship with Julia and his mother, 'Do you think he has touched Julia?' he asked, embarrassingly. Mother studied him for several moments, then offered, 'I'm unsure, Justinian,' She looked like she was about to sob once more.

'Don't get upset about this, I'll get to the bottom of it. Catalina is such an odious person,' he shook his head, cursed. Mother put a hand on his arm in an effort to try and soothe him 'Calm yourself, son, Cassius will know what to do,' Attia said, then, 'Justinian, we need to know what happened to father.'

At dusk, Justinian's mother retired to bed. The villa was abnormally quiet; the three servants were in their own rooms and occupied themselves as noiselessly as possible, aware that the household was in mourning. Justinian sat by himself in the main living room, his mind churning over the day's events, most especially his father's death. A wave of sadness descended over him and frustration began to boil in him. It was up to him to attend to Catalina, find out what he was after. It wasn't a mystery anyway, it being perfectly obvious what Catalina was up to—he was after Julia.

Justinian couldn't imagine his fourteen-year-old sister falling for a rogue such as Catalina. he was possibly ten years older than Justinian. Plus, he had a cohort of ruffians backing him up. No, Justinian couldn't confront him on his own. He needed to speak to some elder. He could visit Scaurus, chief senator, and then his thoughts turned to Lydia, Scaurus's young wife. Would she start tossing him distractions such as herself once again? Justinian had heard talk of her, she was voracious and during Scaurus's absences, she would gather elderly, young, and younger men, in a wilful indulgence of lovemaking. Even women couldn't resist her charms. For Justinian, these were unmentionable subjects, but factual and, possibly ruinous.

Leaving his villa for the Campus Martius, Justinian suddenly swung in the opposite direction. He was heading for Scaurus's villa. Justinian knew he was already in dire straits with the Roman army for being late returning and so an extra hour of absenteeism wouldn't amount to much more punishment. His walk was brisk, and he made it to Scaurus's villa by mid-evening. Not too late, the house servant, with raised eyebrows, admitted Justinian and told him to wait while he consulted with Lady Lydia. Justinian's hopes sunk quickly as he contemplated what might arise with Lydia during the evening. He took her hand and kissed it by way of greeting. Tonight, she was dressed in a white cotton stola with a pretty flounce and a girdle below her bosom. The garment accentuated her tallish figure. Justinian, despite his reservations, considered her an enchanting woman. She looked surprised on seeing him but retained the seductive smile; clearly, she was pleased to see him. 'Why, young man, I'm delighted to see you again. And, again, my husband is absent, at the Senate with Sulla and a few of his cronies.'

'I'm sorry to disturb you, Lady Lydia, but I need to talk to your husband,' he entreated, adding, 'my father has died in Spain fighting Sertorious. Catalina knows of his death and is pestering my mother and sisters. To what end, I'm unsure, but I do know of his reputation.' He added, 'I need to talk to somebody with authority.'

'Oh dear, I'm so sorry to hear about your father, and, that pest, Catalina,' She sighed, but Justinian saw a momentary glance away as she mentioned Catalina, 'He's a devil's brew,' she said, adding, 'and you need to keep him away from your sisters.' She gestured for him to sit on the couch, gently pressing him to move. 'I think, tonight, we will have some wine. You are a soldier now, quite the young warrior.' They settled on the couch. Lydia making sure their bodies were touching; he could feel her warmth and made no effort to move away. Lydia called for her servant who promptly arrived with a jug of wine and two goblets. Justinian considered this a well-rehearsed exercise; Lydia obviously took pleasure in male company.

'Scaurus, I'm sure, will help you. He knows of Catalina—they used to be friends you know, but as soon as Catalina donned the Senate toga, he became a mule-headed moron. Anyway, we'll do our best to stop him harassing your family, especially the girls.'

Justinian was almost about to offer a thank you when Lydia shuffled closer to him; she had a sheepish grin on her face, 'Say your thanks when Catalina has been dealt with,' she explained, 'but, in the meantime, let us two get to know each other a little better,' and shamelessly placed her hand over his toga and lightly squeezed his penis, 'Goodness, you are well endowed!'

Justinian flinched at her brazen touch, but also felt a sense of excitement. His ambivalence was largely due to thinking about Lady Lydia quite a lot over the period he had been at the military camp. An agonising reality had hit him on his sixteenth birthday: he had never had any relationships with females or closeness to girls during his younger years. His household was full of women, but he was always too busy to notice. Watching his younger sisters grow-up had only left him with an impression that girls were silly and scatty. But now, he felt so stirred-up over this mature lady touching him, he trembled, putting his face closer to hers. And for the first time in his life he was actually kissing and not wanting to pull himself away. This was going to be an interesting night, he thought.

And interesting it was, as Lady Lydia almost smothered him trying to get at his army tunic, but he was saved by the loud cough of the servant who had suddenly appeared to inform the lady that the master had arrived home from the Senate. Marcus Aemilianus Scaurus entered the room and eyed the dishevelled Justinian with some suspicion, 'Who's this young chap?' he insisted, making his way to a fruit bowl on the table. Lydia, who had almost been caught at it once more, collected herself and answered, 'Marcus, dear, this is the son, Justinian, of Justinius of the Cornelia, the family have just found out their father's died in Spain, fighting Sertorius. Oh, shame on Sertorius.' Marcus Aemilianus Scaurus frowned at his wife, 'Let the young man speak for himself, Lydia,' he demanded.

It is true senator, and now that we are without a father, Catalina is trying to take advantage of my younger sisters, he…'

'Catalina, you say,' interrupting Justinian, 'the man's scum!' Scaurus spat and approached Justinian; 'Believe you've just joined the army, why are you not wearing your uniform?'

'Sir, we've been ordered not to wear our army garb around the city streets. Marius has lots of followers, and they're out for the blood of anyone associated with Sulla, the young man responded, adding, 'and at this time of night, it's too risky.' Justinian hesitated, shook his head, 'I'm also absent without permission from Mars Field garrison and,' Marcus quickly looked to Lydia, 'Oh, don't worry about that, we can vouch for delaying you. One of our servants can escort you back and issue a signed scroll. They know about your father, I assume?'

'They should know by now.' Justinian answered, relieved about the signed scroll.

Scaurus sighed, sat down on the divan and shook his head, 'Rome's in an awful state, factions killing each other, there's bodies everywhere. Sulla is confiscating properties and putting up proscription lists on the Senate's doors. Tonight, the list has over fifty names, always headed by Marius and his son. It's dreadful, nobody wants to talk or negotiate. Sulla's got Catalina and his misfits doing the dirty work. May the gods spare us.' Lydia moved closer to him and put her hand on his arm as a gesture to calm him, 'Get Lucius to accompany Justinian back to the garrison,' she offered.

Justinian was astonished at the reception he received once he got back at the military camp. Officers on duty commiserated, fellow soldiers sidled up to him and grabbed his shoulders attempting to reassure him that things do get better. No senior officers were available that night, so Justinian leapt on his narrow bunk and fell soundly asleep.

The following days were crammed with activity. Justinian's Vth cohort was ordered to fall in, four abreast and march with a tribune leading. Marius had been sighted just south of Formiae, about seventy-five leagues (105 miles) south of Rome.

Their mission: to bring Marius and his son back to Rome for trial for treason, dead or alive. The march commenced at dawn, the soldiers, weary from too much liberty but, as Roman soldiers tend to do, they marched in step and maintained a hasty pace, their hob-nailed sandals crunching through the early morning stillness, alarming the locals and scattering livestock.

Justinian marched in step with the file of soldiers around him. During the previous weeks, he'd spend a lot of time learning to march correctly. The training marches had been rigorous and lengthy but, the distance to be covered today seemed to him impossible. It would take almost two days to reach Formiae. After a few hours, his back-pack and yoke were digging painfully into his flesh. His breeches chafed his flanks. Justinian started to feel miserable but as he was aware of his comrades marching next to him, he determinedly kept pace and bit down on his lips.

His mind concentrated on his family, his mother and two sisters were vulnerable with Catalina moseying around. However, he felt calm about the circumstances owing to Scaurus's probable intervention. Scaurus was a powerful man, senior senator of the chamber. People respected and upheld his powerful oratory and advice. Catalina would not be fool enough to cross Scaurus. Justinian felt himself flagging; they had been marching for five hours and his body was in the pain. Then, suddenly, the ranks of soldiers halted, and began disbanding. Now they had to prepare a camp.

The site chosen for the camp was next to a gentle stream. For the next period, before dusk, there was a flurry of activity as men set-up palisades, tents, organised and fed the baggage mules, set aside an area for the Command Centre *(principia)*. A number of braziers were heated up and, before long, a warm cosy atmosphere existed throughout the camp, and the smell of roasted meat pervaded everyone's noses. The junior cadet officers, including Justinian, made themselves useful by organising a scouting party to make sure no Marian forces were nearby. Hands on swords, the party split into three groups and scouted around the camp periphery until they were certain the area was safe. As it was, soldiers were already using the stream for washing and relieving themselves.

The scouting groups made their way back to the camp. Justinian held back, he needed to relieve himself. Ensuring he was downstream from the camp, he found a secluded spot among overhanging tree branches. He tore down his breeches and relieved himself. He started to wash when suddenly someone's arm swung across his throat, grabbing him so tightly he couldn't utter a sound. A gruff voice, heavily accented, sounded in his ear, 'Hold your words, son, or you'll die on the spot.'

Justinian tried to nod but was totally overwhelmed by the man's strength' He heard another voice, but it wasn't as harsh, 'Bring him over here, I think I know him.' Suddenly, Justinian, recognised the calmer voice, it was Marius. The brute holding him began to pull him towards the riverbank, 'Come on, and don't struggle, you turd, or I'll put you under.' Justinian complied and began to relax himself as he neared the riverbank. After shuffling up the bank, the tall brute released him. Justinian saw the old general and knelt down next to him; he gazed at him in awe and mumbled something incoherent. 'What did you say?' Marius asked through a thick beard.

'Sorry, sir, I only inquired after your health,' Justinian quickly explained.

'It's good to know someone cares,' Marius declared.

'I listen to your speeches in the Senate,' Justinian stated.

'I'm glad to hear it, though they're not much use now. You watch, in the next few days many senators will disappear. Sulla is a cruel master, he's likely to kill many of my supporters himself,' Marius sighed, adding, 'I feel for Rome, he'll undo all the reforms, the causes of the lower classes will diminish to the extent they will have no voice in governing Rome.'

After swearing an oath that he wouldn't run back to the camp, the trio moved off the riverbank into the forest. Justinian wondered about his own loyalty to Marius. He knew he couldn't tell any of his fellow soldiers of his encounter with the aging general. But, what now, how should he deal with this predicament? How would he manage to return to camp? Once more, he found himself absent without leave. He stumbled on. The giant of a man walking behind him kept pushing him forward, 'Holy Jupiter, won't you stop that!' Justinian shouted, adding 'I've been marching for five hours and I am bloody knackered.' Marius said something to the big fellow; Justinian couldn't recognise the language, but whatever was said, worked. The big fellow left him alone.

After walking for quite some time, they reached a makeshift shelter of branches, ferns and strands of tall grasses. Surprised, Justinian hadn't seen it until he was almost on top of it; Marius drew back a piece of fabric and entered the shelter. Marius's offsider gestured for Justinian to go in next. Once inside, his eyes adjusting to the gloom, he saw that the floor was covered in animal skins including sheep wool. Marius, old and arthritic, moaned as he sat down. He grabbed a large bladder of water and began gulping down copious amounts. Wiping his lips, he handed the bladder to Justinian who drank his fill and handed it to the giant.

'By the way,' Marius whispered, 'this is Theorex, he's a Gaul. He was captured two years ago but I adopted him as one of my guards. He's remained faithful ever since. He won't hurt you unless I tell him to. I speak to him in a Gallic tongue but he speaks sufficient Latin to be understood. He's an ugly brute, eh.' Marius smiled; Justinian did the same while making himself comfortable on the floor.

'We've caught some fish, but we cannot cook it. Your troop of soldiers will likely spot the smoke. We'll eat it raw; I am kind of getting used to eating things raw.' And then, Marius lay himself down and closed his eyes.

Justinian too was exhausted and lay down. Within a short space of time, both were snoring, fast asleep, while Theorex remained awake.

Justinian awoke in total darkness, rubbed his eyes in case he'd turned blind. Shook his head and then slowly he began to make out forms on the floor. It all came flooding back to him, the capture, Marius and the huge brute. Theorex groaned and sat up. He handed Justinian some fish meat and signified that he should chew it. Reluctantly; Justinian placed a piece in his mouth and began chewing. Almost immediately, his stomach churned but once he swallowed, his stomach eased. One could get used to this, he considered, while chewing on a second piece.

Marius stirred, farted, then sat up. He took some fish from Theorex and hastily started chewing.

'Need to have a piss,' Justinian said. Marius spoke to Theorex and motioned that they should go outside. It was a warm night; they were wrapped in total darkness but Justinian relieved himself against a tree with Theorex standing next to him. 'If it's all right, I'm not going to bolt. Besides, I don't know my way back to the camp, and I can't see a bloody thing!' he angrily declared. Theorex simply gave one of his grunts and the pair returned to the shelter.

The remainder of the evening was spent in total darkness. A fire or even a candle was out of the question. Theorex carried flints but all three men knew the risks. Marius was content to talk about himself, his accomplishments, his wife, his son and just about any topic connected with his exploits. Then there was Sulla who, unfairly, stole Marius's plans and decisions, claiming them for himself and becoming a champion of the senatorial faction.

Dawn broke slowly, with still no sign of the men from the nearby camp. Justinian considered his predicament. He wasn't treated like a prisoner, but he obviously wasn't free to go anywhere. He was beginning to like Marius, despite his recent reputation. Some folks believed Marius was insane, but it didn't appear to so.

'Now, what are we going to do with you?' Marius asked, interrupting Justinian's thoughts. The question was meaningless, Justinian shook his head, 'Really don't know, I'm caught up in a feud between two great men, and both of you have acted irresponsibility out of pride. I really don't see any point in taking sides.'

Marius nodded, 'You're quite the diplomat aren't you, and I must admit you are quite a sensible and mature young man. Perhaps you should start off in the Law courts and mix with the likes of Cicero and Cato—yes, perhaps that's your future.'

'I must complete my military training first, it's very important to me,' Justinian acknowledged, 'I've got to achieve my goals one step at a time,' he added.

'Marius nodded, 'Yes, very judicious, just don't make too many enemies along the way. Tell me, are you for the populares or are you a sympathiser for the Nobles?'

'At this stage, I'm neither. My only consideration is Rome herself.'

'Hmm, I like what I'm hearing. If I let you go. Will you inform on me?'

'No, I'll simply say I got lost and spent the night in a woodcutter's cottage. They'll have no reason to doubt my word.'

'I'm sure they won't,' and for the first time, Marius smiled, but it didn't last; a serious look now masked his countenance, 'I'm sorry to hear about your father. I knew him, not well, mind you, but I found him to be a conscientious soldier. It's a pity he fell in with Sulla's bullies, and then was sent off with Metellus to fight my good friend, Sertorious. Fortuna is a cruel mistress.'

Justinian's face mirrored consternation, 'You mean Sertorious was one of your own.'

Marius nodded, 'One of my best centurions.' Marius's eyes glazed, he bowed his head, adding, 'after our victories over the Teutons and the Ambrones, Sertorious became disillusioned over the army command. Sulla had a hand in that.'

Justinian could only shake his head in acknowledgement. After some moments, he looked glumly at Marius, 'I must get a move on if I'm to catch up with my troop of soldiers. We're marching to Formiae to follow up a sighting of you. Where do you intend to go?'

Marius studied Justinian's face for several moments, 'I'm meeting a vessel to take me to Greece, then on to Bithynia with the old monarch, Nicomedes.'

'Be careful, sir, Sulla's in league with Mithridates, and he's has eyes everywhere.' With that, the youth bid farewell to Marius and Theorex and exited the shelter.

After walking some distance towards the river, Justinian finally reached the main road, the Via Appia, which stretched all the way to Capua, in the south of Italy. Formiae could only be about another day away, he hoped, and turned towards the south and started walking.

Whilst walking, Justinian considered his immediate problems. Agrippa, his commanding officer would deem him a deserter, the penalty for this is usually death. But he was sure, Agrippa would give him the benefit of the doubt, desertion could be easily explained by losing his way in the forest. After all, he was returning for duty. His next problem was his sword and helmet. He had left them on the riverbank before he initially entered the water. The sword, helmet, army issue, was a problem—he would probably have to pay for it.

Next, he considered his stance on Marius and Sulla. This was a conundrum, his father fought in Sulla's army and now he was following suit. Sulla is evil, Marius had told him. Sulla wanted to remove the hard-fought power from the plebs; they could have no say in the Roman Senate. No voice in reforms, no veto to protect their interests. These actions by Sulla would only serve to subjugate the lower classes, and that, he felt, was wrong.

The solitary figure of Justinian quietly walked down the Via Appia towards Formiae; donkey drawn carts and wagons often passed him going in the opposite direction towards Rome. By dusk, he was informed by an old man on a wagon full of cabbages—that's in another day he would reach Formiae. He continued his journey, heading south. After a short period, he saw a figure approaching, leading a pony. As they got closer, he judged the figure to be that of a youth, wearing an excessive amount of clothing for this time of the year. Almost passing each other, Justinian noticed the amount of hair sticking out the sides of the person's hood. He nodded to the person, saying, 'Pleasant sort of a day, m'lady.' She pulled up suddenly, stared daggers at him, then spoke; 'Why do you call me m'lady?' Her voice even sounded lady-like.

'Oh,' Justinian stammered, feeling the sting in her voice, 'I said that after seeing the length of your hair.' He added. 'I'm sorry, I meant no disrespect.' They were now facing each other, and Justinian studied her face, the skin flawless and her eyes, large, brown and defiant, 'Right, so you're not a woman but a man with long hair, just like the Germanic tribesmen. And, I presume you're here to report back on our military might, eh.'

'Oh, you silly soldier, I'm no such thing. I'm merely taking my pony to a safer keep and,' she paused, 'and, yes, I am a girl, my name is Penelope. I dress this way because I fear men may try to molest me. It's happened to me before.'

Justinian felt embarrassed, nodded, 'Jupiter! I'm sorry. Yes, I should have realised your vulnerability. Please forgive me.'

She studied his face, 'Yes, I forgive you. You look so sorrowful, how could I not forgive you?' Then she added, 'Would you like something to eat? Let's get off the road and go over there.' With the pony in tow, they swung off the road to a secluded area in the edge of the forest.

'Ye merciful gods, I'm so hot. Let me get this shawl off, we can sit on it,' the shawl came off and she laid it, pressed it flat, and invited him to sit down. He noticed she was still wearing two white cotton coveralls stuffed into a pair of breeches, 'No wonder, you're so hot,' he said with raised eyebrows.'

With the pony secured to a branch, the pair shared some of her biscuits, and water from a bladder which the pony had carried. For the second time in as many days, Justinian found himself eating with somebody he'd never had a decent conversation with in the past. 'So, where do you call home?' He asked.

'Inland from Formiae,' she replied with difficulty, her mouth full of biscuit. 'Oops, sorry, I should have waited, your mouth is full.' he responded, clumsily.

She waved her hand, 'No matter,' and swallowed the last of the biscuit. She went on to explain where her home was located, and how poor she and her mother were. Her father had died five years ago from chills on the chest. Her and her mother couldn't afford to look after the pony. Her mother was going to sell it but she had taken it early this morning and was searching for some place to shelter the animal.

'You know you'll have to pay a fee for the animal's keep,' Justinian said.

'Yes, I know. I thought if I were nearer to Rome, I could perhaps get work as a scullery maid or servant, or something,' she started showing signs of becoming sullen. Justinian felt for her, 'Yes, there are plenty of opportunities in Rome to get work.'

She continued to talk about her miserable background. Her home was a run-down, old stone building that was once storage for flour bags. She and her mother rented it cheaply from a flour merchant. 'That's fortunate,' he commented. She looked at him as if she were about to rebuke him. 'He charges cheap rent because we do other things for him like favours.' Justinian looked puzzled. She went on, 'Sexual favours.' He was shocked, didn't know what to say. So, she continued to relate how poor she and her mother were, how they danced and sang for a few coins each night in the inns. Her father had really died in a drunken brawl. Justinian frowned and said sorry. She quickly added, 'mother and I are not; he was a drunken brute.' After a short period of quiet reflection, both brooding over their own predicaments, she studied the trees and said, 'I'll tell you the truth about the pony now. I'm sure I can trust you.' Justinian made himself more comfortable on the shawl and braced himself for the truth about the pony.

'The pony belongs to the flour merchant, the same man who owns the dilapidated building they lived in. The flour merchant is always cruel to the pony. The animal was always tied to big cylindrical stone and had to go round and round to grind the grain. I just couldn't stand seeing the animal being whipped. Before dawn, I unhitched the pony and we started walking towards Rome. This is where I'm at.'

'There are usually serious penalties for stealing livestock,' he commented.

'But what about cruelty to animals?' She replied.

Justinian admired her simple approach to things, but felt she was being naive. Now that she had told him the truth about the pony, he'd have to avoid being implicated in the theft of the animal. He shook his head; how did he manage to get in these messes?

He smiled at her, admired her childlike solutions to things. 'I do believe you, and, anyway, I could see the old scarring on the pony's back. Yes, it's a shame having cruel people in the world.'

'Anyway, I'm glad you believe me. At least I know you're on my side. Anyway, what's your name?'

'Justinian of the Cornelius.

'That sounds posh, is your family rich?' She asked.

'No, my family is not rich, my father was an officer in the army with the Mettelae, fighting in Spain but he died.

'Who was he fighting against?'

'Sertorious, and his rebels.'

'I'm sorry about your father. she offered.

'I didn't know him well, he was always away.'

'Any brothers or sisters?'

'Two sisters, younger than me.'

'I bet they spoil you,' she offered with a grin.

'Not really, I don't have much to do with them. They usually spoil mother.'

She yawned noisily, 'Oh, I'm so tired.'

'Why not have a sleep; I'll keep an eye on you. Just lie down here, I won't abandon you.'

'Yes, all right. Make sure the pony's tied-up properly.'

She lay down. Justinian studied her for a few moments, then rose up and strode over to the pony, checked his rein, he was secure and busily chewing on the ground cover.

Justinian felt depressed over his supposed desertion. He badly needed to communicate his circumstances to an officer. Not only was he in trouble with military command but, he was also in trouble with his comrades. For some moments, he considered the wisdom of reaching his comrades in Formiae. Or, perhaps he should go back to the garrison and face the music there. He could then escort Penelope some of the way to find a stable for her pony.

It was then that he heard horses galloping, Penelope screamed. Justinian swung around and watched the horses slow down to a canter and veer to the left towards the pair. Justinian then saw Penelope bolt towards a dense area of the forest, leaving her pony tied to the branch. The horses came to a halt near Justinian. Alarmed, he rushed over to the pony which was jumping wildly from the commotion. Justinian threw his arm around the panicked animal's neck, 'Whoa! Whoa! There's a good boy, whoa!' The pony bucked a couple of times then started to settle.

One of the horsemen kicked his steed and followed the girl into the forest. 'What is going on?' Justinian hollered, holding the pony by its rope rein One of the riders looked intently at the youth, 'Are you a soldier?' he demanded. Justinian nodded, 'Yes, but I lost my troop,' he answered. The rider, a mature middle-aged man got down from his mount. 'Are you in league with that girl?'

'No, sir, I met her on the Via Appia. We were walking in opposite directions. I'm after my soldier comrades, probably at Formiae by now,' he explained, then added, 'What exactly is the problem?'

'The pony belongs to me, she stole it this morning,' he uttered angrily, 'I want it back and I want her charged and fined.'

'She's only young, sir, what if we can compensate you for the pony's absence?' Justinian offered.

‘I’ve lost a mornings work, the pony operates the grain crusher, I’ve probably lost about three denarii in total. How are you going to pay this?’

‘I’m not sure, sir,’ then Justinian’s eyes lit up, ‘she could work it off, kitchen duties, maid or laundress, sir,’

‘My dear man, I cannot trust her. She does have a reputation around Formiae. If I’m to employ her she must change her ways and show some initiative,’ he looked past Justinian, ‘Markus has her; she’ll answer for her reckless behaviour,’

‘Don’t be too harsh sir, from what she tells me she’s from a poor family on a small unproductive farm.’

‘She’s lying; she’s simply a whore and dances for soldiers who tip her. By the way, what name did she give you? The horseman asked; a bemused look on his face.

‘She said her name was Penelope, sir.’

‘Ha, there you go another lie, a fanciful one at that, the wife of Ulysses, I doubt it. She just cannot be trusted.’

Justinian swung around, stared at the struggling girl, her arms locked behind her back, the horsemen pushing her towards them.

‘Sir, I beg you, go easy on her, she’s only a youngster,’ Justinian shouted. The man quickly turned his head; a bloody scratch ran upwards from his lower jaw to under his eye. ‘If she’s only a youngster, how did I get this?’

Justinian gasped, ‘Ye gods,’ he uttered. He turned back to the mounted horseman, ‘I don’t know what to think, she gave me a totally different impression. What’s her real name?’

‘It’s Sabina, and she’s a tramp,’ the man angrily replied, ‘and I’m going to give her some of her own medicine.’ He looked over to the third man now holding the pony. He nodded once then directed his attention to Justinian. The Pony man tied the beast to a branch then slowly ambled over to the youth. This man was big, his face scarred, probably an ex-soldier, or gladiator and his right eye was opaque. Before Justinian could do anything, the man swung a fist into the side of the youth's head. Justinian dropped like a rock to the ground, out cold.

The mounted man shouted at the other two, 'Do what you will with her but leave her alive, for me.' He dismounted, strolled over to Justinian and studied the youth. His pushed the youth's body sideways with his foot. He figured the youth wouldn't be seeing daylight for some time.

Sabina screamed as the men forced her into a cope of bushes. The ex-soldier was the first to drop to the ground next to her. She screamed again but couldn't push him away. After a few screams, she simply sobbed and called out for her mother. It was a short period, and then the two men were finished with her and left her moaning on the ground, her lower torso covered in blood. The third man, the landowner, knelt by the girl's heaving body, then softly cupped her breasts, 'You stupid bitch,' he whispered, then put his hands around her neck.

Daylight came gradually to Justinian; at first, he couldn't focus his eyes, everything a blur. After a while, branches formed against the sky, then leaves. And suddenly he was fully conscious and remembered the last thing that happened to him. 'Ye gods!' he moaned and rubbed the side of his head, 'Ouch!' He cautiously sat up and immediately thought of Sabina. He called her name, no response. Wearily, he got to his feet; looked around, noticed the pony was gone and assumed the horsemen had left too. Had they taken Sabina too?

He walked around their eating site, casting his gaze into forest for signs of Sabina. Despite the theft of the pony, he couldn't help but like her and to some extent, he felt sorry for her. Justinian pulled-up sharply, 'Oh no!' he exclaimed, sighting her bare leg amongst the growth and so he frantically rushed towards the copse. Frantically snatching the undergrowth, he cleared the area around the prone girl, all the while muttering curses and profanities. Finally, he stood over the body. Shocked and breathless, he couldn't quite grasp what he was seeing. She was lying with her head to one side, her lower torso naked and covered in blood. Justinian slumped down next to her looking for signs of breathing, there were none. He knew about pulses and felt her wrist, nothing; her flesh was cool to touch. Suddenly, he reeled back in horror, gasping and groaning. Apart from bodies of nobodies lying in the streets of Rome, this was the first occasion of knowing somebody dead. He started gagging, wanting desperately to vomit. Quickly getting back on his feet, he hastily made his way to the Via Appia, hoping to find someone for help.

Once on Via Appia, Justinian started walking south in the direction of Rome. His mind awhirl with conflicting thoughts, he walked slowly, aimlessly along the road. The sun was setting and possibly only an hour of daylight remaining. He knew there would be no traffic in the night owing to the prevalence of bandits and drunkards. He came upon a stone distance marker on the side of the road and sat on it, and waited.

Chapter 2

Julia considered herself pretty and, at fifteen, believed she was undergoing some sort of bodily change. She was considered tall for a girl, slim, somewhat gangly, with a chiselled face, big bright eyes and a wide mouth with full lips. Her dark, longish hair encircled an olive complexion. Men gave her a second glance and she felt good about this. Despite the awful news of her father, her mind was fully occupied with her budding friendships. She believed she was in love with Catalina, a young patrician senator. He was twice her age, but on the three occasions of being in his presence; she sensed his steads gaze was examining her. Julia knew of his reputation, but didn't care. She was of an age where conceited behaviour and unfettered promiscuity went hand in hand in Republican Rome. Julia simply fitted in with the norms of society but had kept quiet about it with her family. She also kept quiet about today's venue, taking place in one of Rome's seedier districts, the Castra Urbana. She would travel in company with ten or more fellow supplicants, attending a Bacchanalia festivity of gluttony and drunkenness, ending with the usual lapse into debauchery. Julia was considered a minor so was restricted to watered wine and could not partake of the later depraved sessions. However, she could remain an observer, which pleased her. She enjoyed the alluring antics of men and women, the total abandon of values and virtue.

There were three other females of the same age in her group and were keen to partake of the rituals when they reached the age of eighteen. Together, the group of four was street smart, knew the districts well, and often had escorts of one or two soldiers. Julia was a wily young lady and had managed to keep her secrets to herself; not even Antonia was privy.

Today, there was a sense of relief for the mob in Rome's Subura. Only the equestrian and patrician orders still held fears as to what Sulla planned. His soldiers were still hunting for Marius and his son. In fact, Julia believed her brother belonged to a military troop searching for the old fuddy-duddy ex-consul, up north somewhere.

Berenice, Aelia and Dalmatia, her three companions, joined the small procession and immediately all thoughts of her soldier brother and her father's deaths were dismissed. The four girls giggled with guarded whispers as they greeted each other, then commiserations were directed at Julia over her family loss. She adopted a facade of grief and thanked her companions for being so thoughtful. However, today there were more pressing matters to consider, and the banter continued. Together, each of the girls decided to shun the wearing of undergarments for the day's festivities so each of the girls, in turn, lifted the hem of their stola to reveal white, naked fleshy backsides. These actions took place when nobody was paying them any attention, and the giggles resumed. It was their group secret for the Bacchanalia.

There was quite a gathering at the Castra Urbana and the rituals were under way. The group, now consisting of four females and three males, quickly made it through the gate onto the common. There were strict rules about the proportion of women to men, the group passed the scrutiny. Once on the common, they began mingling with participants and were surprised to see people they knew of. It was nearing dusk, so hundreds of torches were lit, producing a spectacular effect. Two high-priestesses walked among the crowd, intoning, using an old Greek language that most of the revelers couldn't understand. Men and women began cavorting with each other, waving their arms about and touching each other. The girls, now in a sizeable spectator group, looked on in rapt interest. Several men, most probably gladiators, naked, began strolling through the crowd of spectators, displaying their ramrod penises. Women began swooning and rushing to get near them so they could touch the men's swellings. Amphorae of wine were beginning to empty as the crowd built up. Certain areas on the common were so crowded that individuals were falling and being crushed; screams could be heard.

After the priestesses completed their chanting, the signal was given for the held torches to be doused in the Tiber. The torch bearers slowly made their way through the throng of revelers to the riverbank. In the low light Julia could see couples having sex, men with men, women with women and men with women. It seemed as if a giant orgy were taking place before her very eyes. She suddenly recalled the reason for the Bacchannial festival: fertility, wine, freedom, intoxication and ecstasy and the initiates were certainly reveling in everything. Julia was starting to feel heady from the wine, Berenice had fallen asleep and the other girls had disappeared into the crowd. Julia was now sitting on the grass, her stola draped over her knees and she knew her posture and sitting positions had to be done with care. Men crossing in front were looking for willing partners and they stared at her, even eyeing Berenice. Julia knew she must remain alert, not only for herself, but also for sleepy Berenice.

There were shouts coming from the crowds on the riverbank. These partakers were the initiated and the stood next to the torch-bearers. At a given command by the high-priestess, who wore a shawl and a mask so nobody could identify her, the torch-bearers slowly lowered their torches into the water, pushing the burning tips under. All the torches seem to extinguish at once, sending the area by the river into darkness. A collective groan issued from the separate crowds of onlookers and initiates. The high-priestess issued another command and the torch-bearers slowly lifted their wooden shafts out of the water and immediately, the shafts burst into flames once more. Cries of astonishment issued from the crowds. Julia gasped at the spectacle, as did hundreds of others, they didn't know about the combination of sulphur and magnesium, combined in a hardened paste. With prayers officially over, a cacophony of cymbals and drums, accompanied by horns and pipes, erupted.

Julia tried to awaken Berenice but couldn't, and decided the poor girl was stupidly drunk. How to get her home would be the next problem. Julia thought it so unfair; it was now her responsibility to look after one of her friends. While thinking along these lines, a man's voice behind her said, 'Hello, Julia.' She swung around and found herself facing Catalina. He was dressed in a preposterous costume, 'Do you like it, Julia? I'm supposed to be Sol Invictus.' Julia wanted to giggle. Catalina was dressed in a gold, tight-fitting costume with a short skirt, a hat designed like the sun with golden rays extending upwards. He dropped down near her and made himself comfortable. She drew in a sharp intake of breath as his short skirt stretched back along his thighs and she glimpsed his thick penis. He couldn't see her deep blush in the darkness but knew that he'd made a favourable impression. 'Julia, I've made love to four beautiful women tonight. I would like to make love to you.'

Julia shook her head and stammered, 'No you won't, I'm under age. The high-priestess forbids it, its anathema.'

'Oh, who cares about rules at this sort of celebration, come on Julia, we can do it here, now. I can tell you are naked underneath; you're yearning for it.' Julia felt her desires almost overpowering her. Catalina's face was a mask of determination. He added, 'Look around, couples are fucking each other all over the common, don't forget this is also a celebration of ecstasy,' and he placed his hand on her right breast. Julia flinched, tried to grab his hand and pull it away. Catalina leapt at her from his sitting position and pinned her wrists down on the grass. 'There now, I'll give you what you want, and when I finish with you, I'll fuck your sleeping friend too,' he declared. He released one of her wrists and ran his hand from her ankle the length of her leg until he reached her bush, then cupped her privy. Julia squirmed, slammed her knees together, attempting to obstruct his groping hand, but the sudden pleasure of his touch was too much for her and she groaned with delight.

Chapter 3

Justinian woke with a start, recollected why he'd chosen to lie in the corpse with the dead girl and shuddered. He had returned to her because he couldn't leave her body to be ravaged by animals throughout the night. He had covered her with branches and lain next to her. With a new day dawning, he felt the morning chill, wrapped his arms around his chest and promptly moved towards the roadway, determined to get help.

Though it was very early in the morning, a steady stream of carts and wayfarers on horseback travelled in both directions on the "Via Appia". Merchants heading to Rome for the markets would be his best chance; he decided and approached a horse drawn cart. The man steering the horse looked at him suspiciously and picked up his whip, clearly not in the mood for trouble but, he did tug the reins, stopping the horse, 'What can I do for you, son?' This would be the tricky bit, Justinian knew, so he had to frame his statement so as not to alarm the driver. 'Excuse me, sir, but I need some help. Er, a young woman has been murdered in the forest, just over there,' he pointed.

'Ye gods, son, are you serious?' The driver challenged.

‘Sir, I am serious and must get her body back to Rome to the authorities. I am a soldier of the IVth legion and I plead, sir, that you render some assistance,’ Justinian demanded in an authoritative voice. The driver, incredulous, simply stared at the youth. ‘Sir, I’m pleading with you for help; we cannot leave her in the forest for animals to tear her apart. She needs a proper burial but the authorities need to know who the murderers are,’ Justinian maintained.

The driver shook his head, ‘there’s some room on the cart, we’ll need to wrap her up. Do you know when she died?’

‘Yesterday, the culprits knocked me out, see here,’ Justinian showed the man the bruising around his temple, ‘I was escorting her back to Rome,’ he added, not mentioning the stolen pony.

The driver guided his horse and cart carefully between the trees, following the youth, he said, ‘I can see there’s been horses through here, look how they’ve flattened the undergrowth.’

‘Yes, there were three of them’

The pair gently laid Sabina’s body onto the cart. It was wrapped in layers of sacking material, suitably covered. The old horse chewed on the ground cover, seemed to be enjoying the respite. The cart owner, nervous, kept uttering prayers and chants as the two readied for the trip into Rome, which would take most of the morning. Clearly the driver was a superstitious fellow. One aspect of concern for Justinian was the wearing of a partial army uniform. Any troop of soldiers passing them on the road would suspect him of being a deserter and that would be disastrous. It wasn’t long before they came across a tavern. The driver agreed to purchase an old blanket for the horse. He got one and threw it up to the youth, who immediately covered his partial uniform, and was thankful for the bit of warmth it provided.

Before long, they were passing more buildings, the outskirts of Rome. The sun was directly above so it was close to midday. The Appian Gate loomed large after a further long spell on the road. 'Where do you want to take the lass, son? I've got to pick up vegetables from the market near the forum,' the driver declared.

'I have to report to the garrison first, then the urban prefect, and then probably a magistrate,' Justinian replied, anticipating the driver's angry reaction.

'Now look, lad, I've no time to go traipsing all over the city with this body of yours. You'll have to find a place to put the lassie, then attend to my business. I agreed to help you get the body to the city and I've done that.'

'Yes. Yes, I know, and I'm thankful, let's just go to the garrison and I'll see what can be done,' Justinian replied, wearily.

The garrison, located on the Field of Mars, was crowded with soldiers and horses. Preparations were taking place for Sulla's triumph, his parade through the city with the bounty of his campaigns in the east against Mithradates. The parade would also include a number of prisoners who would likely be strangled afterwards. They parked the horse and cart outside the guard's office, Justinian removed his blanket and made his way to the command tent. Sentries outside the tent eyed him suspiciously due to the missing aspects of his uniform. He explained his misfortunes as brief as he could, the guards allowed him access to the prefect of the guards.

The prefect's deputy, a centurion, listened to Justinian's tale of woe and promptly had him arrested for desertion. The youth, protesting angrily, was manhandled by two guards and dragged into a small area at the rear of the tent, manacled, then chained to a pole. There were two other detainees sitting quietly against their poles, their expressions forlorn and frightened, they too were only youngsters. Justinian ceased his bitter outbursts once he sighted the other apparatus sticking in the ground; it looked like a crucifix but smaller, a whipping stock. He slumped down against his own pole, bowed his head from a sense of hopelessness and shed a few tears.

Meanwhile, a senior guard approached the horse and cart and told the driver to take the body to the senior magistrate's premises near the forum. The girl would have a public burial in an area put aside for the city's abandoned and nameless wretches. The driver grunted, steered his cart towards the Subura. His intentions were to find a quiet alleyway and dump the girl's body. It wasn't his responsibility to look after the deceased girl. And besides, she was taking up too much space on his cart.

Chapter 4

Julia was sore and worn-out but, thankfully, she was going home in a litter that Catalina had organised. He was thoughtful like that, but not thoughtful in love-making. He had handled her roughly, done things to her that she didn't know were normally done to females. Julia had learned the art of love-making through wanton abandon and sheer debauchery. But she shook her head; there was delightful pleasure to be had via the art of love-making.

Catalina had ravaged Berenice too, while she was still half asleep. The man was a literal sex fiend.

Her major problem now was getting back into her bedroom at the villa without her mother finding out. Since father's death, mother has become a recluse and confined herself to her workroom. Antonia wasn't a problem; she knew Julia was going out for the night and didn't ask any questions. Antonia was becoming a bit of a scholar and was reading Thucydides; this irked Julia but she never said anything to upset her younger sister, she was too valuable an ally.

As Julia exited the litter, she suddenly realised that her plans were foiled. Several soldiers were milling around outside the front entrance to her villa. She patted down her stola, and rushed past the soldiers through the front doorway, colliding with the guard officer. 'Oh, uh, so sorry,' she offered by way of a weak apology.

The officer nodded, 'Oh, it was my fault, please accept my apology. Look, I've been talking to your mother about, uh, your brother Justinian. I'm sorry to have to tell you this but he's been charged with desertion.'

Julia gasped, 'What, no, he couldn't have, he…' The officer began noticing the dirty stola, particularly the grass stains. Julia, quickly grasping the situation, blurted, 'I had to sit on the grass to watch the festival last night so I'm a bit messy; it was a long celebration.'

'What festival was that?' the officer quickly asked.

'The Bacchannial, there were hundreds of people there. It was very good,' she explained, hoping he wouldn't make any further inquiries.

He frowned, was about to ask something but changed his mind. 'I told your mother that your brother will face a tribunal in about three days' time. As he is a Roman citizen, second class, he's entitled to counsel so your mother should organise to get a counsellor appointed for him.'

'Thank you, officer, I'll organise that with mother.'

'Oh, and by the way, my condolences, uh, about your father.'

'It's appreciated, now I must see how mother is, goodbye officer.'

Julia headed straight for the bedroom she shared with Antonia. Not surprisingly, she found her younger sister sitting on a stool reading a scroll, 'Don't worry, sister, you're not in trouble,' Antonia offered, adding, 'mother's gone into a trance; she just stares at her bedroom wall. She cannot believe what's happened to Justinian.'

Julia sighed, felt her frustrations dissolve, 'Oh dear, poor mother, I don't believe brother would desert,' she flopped onto her bunk, 'and father, it's all too much for mater. I shall go and see her.'

'You should change first, look at your stola. Where did you spend the night, in the fields?' Antonia offered sombrely, then, 'but more importantly, who did you spend the night with?'

'Oh damn it sister, don't be so cruel. I'm so sore and weary, Catalina is such a beast,' Julia hesitated, then whispered seriously, 'I am no longer a virtuous young woman. Oh gods, what have I done?' She started sobbing, 'Catalina has ruined me.'

Antonia almost said, 'You have ruined yourself,' but held her tongue and rose off the stool, put down her scroll and sat down next to Julia. She put her arm around her sister, saying, 'Julia, losing one's virtue is not the real problem, the risk of pregnancy's the problem, let's hope…' Julia interrupted and between sobs, replied, 'He didn't allow his seed into me, he pulled out at the last moment. Oh, ye gods, I'm a tramp!'

Julia vigorously washed herself and put on a clean cotton shift. Before entering her mother's mom, she took some deep breaths.

'Oh, mother, what has befallen our family? Now our brother is in serious trouble, we need to contact Cassius, he's a magistrate,' she said with an authoritative tone. Her mother sat on her bed and silently stared at the wall, didn't budge. Julia faced her and gently shook her shoulders, 'Mother, you must, ah, we must face the consequences and get help for Justinian. Something is seriously wrong with this situation. Our brother is not a coward. Mother, look at me!' Julia exclaimed, and gently slapped the side of her face. Attia reacted, gasped and looked at Julia.

Justinian was ordered to stand up. A guard unchained him from the pole and he was led into the prefect's tent. The deputy checked his name and rank, then had him stand inside a section of the tent reserved for the prefect. He waited inside for a longish period until he heard the commotion of guards snapping to attention. Justinian stood at attention and bowed his head as the prefect walked into his office. 'Now, what's all this palaver about you deserting your troop?' The officer asked. Justinian instantly looked up and faced Agrippa. 'Oh, sir, am I glad to see you. I didn't desert, sir,' he pleaded. Agrippa motioned for him to sit down, adding, 'Now let's start from the beginning, what happened?'

Justinian related how, after finishing setting up camp, he walked to the stream bank to relieve himself. He left his sword and helmet on the bank and waded into the stream. He peed then decided to go for a swim. He swam for quite some time, not realising he'd drifted some distance from where he entered the stream. Getting back to bank, he then made his way to the Via Appia and met the girl and the pony. After chatting they walked some distance towards the forest. Agrippa frowned at Justinian. 'Sir, it was purely to have something to eat without being disturbed.'

'Yes, I believe you, carry on,' Agrippa answered. So, Justinian explained how the three horsemen arrived and one man, clearly the overseer, claimed that the pony belonged to him. The girl had fled into the forest but one of the men chased her. Another of the men struck me, knocked me out cold. I later regained consciousness and found the girl dead; she had been raped. I felt I should get her back to the proper authorities for burial and also report the incident.'

'Well, it's commendable of you for your concern, but you made a serious error of judgment by getting involved with the girl in the first place. Your first duty is to your fellow soldiers.' Agrippa suddenly adopted a mask of concern, 'You will be charged, but I think it'll be the lesser charge of being absent without permission; the penalty for this could be a fine, or confined to the garrison for a period of time.'

'Yes, sir, I understand,' nodded Justinian, looking a bit uncomfortable. Agrippa studied the youngster for a short period, 'Tell me something, and I want you to be truthful.'

Justinian sighed, 'Yes, sir.'

'I get the feeling that you omitted something important from your incident report. Is this true?'

The youth remained quiet for a short period, then said, 'Before I met the girl, I was held overnight by Marius and one of his Teuton slaves.' He hesitated to let the news sink in. 'But Marius let me go if I promised not to reveal his location, sir.'

But, instead of anger, Agrippa smiled, 'Haha, the old devil, himself.' He frowned, adding, 'spent six years as one of Marius's soldiers. I find it difficult to dismiss him as an enemy of the State. This bitterness between Marius and Sulla has to cease for the benefit of the republic, and having said this, you didn't hear those statements, understood.'

'Certainly sir, I too find it difficult to condemn Marius, or his son,' Justinian offered, and then went on, 'I remained with Marius and his slave overnight. He let me leave in the morning.'

'Did he tell you what his plans are?'

‘No sir, but I feel he’s waiting for a boat to take him to Athens,’ the youth answered.

‘Let’s drop this conversation; ’there are too many ears around here. You can return to your quarters until this business is cleared up. Your mother’s been informed and, I believe she is asking Cassius to defend you. By the way, I was sorry to hear about your father.’

‘Do you know what happened to my father, sir?’

‘All I know is that there was a skirmish with some Iberians and ten or more Roman soldiers were killed by archers. Your father was leading the scouting group.’

Justinian stood to attention and provided Agrippa with a smart salute, about turned and walked out of the garrison. Once outside, Justinian felt a sense of relief and sadness and made his way back to his tent.

Attia pinched her cheeks, trying to get some colour in her face. Despite this, she still had an unhealthy pallor about her. Being cooped-up in her bedroom for the last three days had not been beneficial. The agonies of now being a widow and, with her son in military detention had been extremely trying. Thankfully, Julia had risen to the occasion and comforted, as well as, fortified, Attia. Now she was ready to seek help for her son.

Julia entered the bedroom, watched her mother attempting to apply stibium eyeliner. She thought her mother still possessed a good body shape despite bearing children, and she was pretty with a full bosom. Men would find her attractive, and after a period of mourning, she could marry a rich Roman. So, there were endless possibilities, despite the gloom. Mother turned and faced Julia, asked, 'There Julia, how do I look?'

Julia ignored he paleness, 'You look charming mother. I'm sure you'll win Cassius over to our cause. He's always been fond of you, you know.'

'Oh, Julia stop talking rubbish, you know he's been happily married to Aelia for almost twenty years. Fancies me, what rot!'

Despite her rebuke, Julia smiled, 'You can deny it as much as you like but Cassius is itching to get at you.'

'Julia, you're disgusting! Now get the two servants to escort me to his villa.'

Cassius sat at his marble table and tried to concentrate on what his client was telling him, 'You see, sir, he disputed the volume of wine I sold him. It was the best Valerian I could get my hands on, six amphorae and the rogue claimed one of the amphorae was only half full. I checked each of them before I shipped them to his tavern.'

'What about the person who transported the goods, could he have tampered with the contents?' Cassius asked, trying to suppress a yawn.

'Oh, no sir, Phidius has transported goods for me for years,' the Client insisted, 'I trust him; Phidius knows it's worth his job if I ever caught him pilfering.'

'But all the same there is the possibility isn't there?' Cassius claimed, adding, 'Anyway what is the tavern owner going to do?'

'He wants me up before the magistrate on a charge of fraudulent business practice. I mean to say, this'll ruin me sir.'

‘Yes, yes, let me have the landlord’s details and talk to him. Let’s see if he has any proof to support his accusation. I’ve a feeling the magistrate will throw this allegation out.’ And, so, the conversation between Cassius and his client lingered on for short while. After the client departed, Cassius was told that Attia wanted to talk to him.

Keen to see her, he ushered her into his office, ‘My dear Attia, I’m so sorry to hear about your husband. Please sit here on the divan. He sat next to her, a little too close for comfort. ‘Now, my dear, what is it that I can help you with?’ Attia related what the guard officer told her about Justinian. Cassius was dismayed and equally regretful on hearing the news about Attia’s husband. ‘Oh dear, dear, this is sad news Attia, your son will inherit the property rights so, I imagine you’ll continue to live in your villa.’

‘Now, about Justinian, of course I’ll defend him if it comes to a trial, but I should think there is some plausible reason why he did what he did. I need to talk to him as soon as possible; I’ll visit him in the next day or two. For the moment, shall we have some wine, a little fortification, so to speak?’ Attia nodded her assent.

Chapter 5

By the turn of the first century BC, the metropolis of Rome had a population of almost a million souls. Villas, ranging in size, were for the rich and well-to-do. The bulk of the population lived in *insulae*, tenement blocks, sometimes as high as five floors. These buildings were crammed with people and were located in the areas known as "sublime." Generally, the poorer you were, the higher up you would live in the tenements. Sometimes, up to ten people would live in two small rooms. Conditions were unhygienic, unhealthy and unpalatable. Conditions deteriorated rapidly during the night hours. Ruffians, vagabonds, drunks and prostitutes thrived during the dark night hours.

A frail girl of eight, Davina, had to sit and look out her top floor vent at the world passing by her insula. She was alone in the small room; her mother was out doing some sort of domestic chores for another family. Her father had disappeared several years ago, and her two older brothers were scavenging at the fish markets. It was just after dawn when she noticed a horse drawn cart enter her front laneway. The man steering the horse reined back on the animal and jumped down from the cart, then walked to the rear of the cart and dragged a large, heavy bundle off the wooden floor, carrying it with difficulty to the lane walkway and dumping the bundle outside a vacant warehouse. Davina recognised the man; she had seen him many times with his horse and cart, carrying loads of vegetables. The youngster was curious and decided to go down to the street and look at the bundle when the man got on his way.

She removed some of the covering from the bundle and gasped as a girl's face was exposed. Jerking backwards, she almost fell over. The bundled girl was fast asleep with her eyes open, her face a strange colour. Momentarily transfixed, Davina wondered what she should do next. It was still very early and no people about. Then she quickly about-faced, ran across the narrow road back to her insula and dashed into one of the ground floor vendors. She screamed for Demetrius until the corpulent merchant rushed into his shop space, screaming. 'What's happened, what's wrong, is there a fire?' On seeing the young girl, he come to an abrupt halt, 'Oh, it's you Davina, what's wrong?' he asked her.

Together, they stared at the bundle, 'Oh Jupiter! She can't stay here. Once it gets warm, she'll stink and, yes, she's dead,' Demetrius confirmed, forgetting he was talking to an eight-year-old child. 'I'll get some of the vigils to take her body away.' The vigils, a volunteer band of peacekeepers whose only weapon was a thick length of stick to beat heads with, had no jurisdiction from the law body, the Senate, but they had permission from the locals. The vigils were often involved in protection rackets for revenue.

People and horses were beginning to fill the streets now. Demetrius took Divina's hand and walked back across the road, then turned left instead of right. 'Where we going, Demetrius?' Divina asked.

'To see some friends about the body. They'll look after it,' he replied, keeping his statements as simple as possible.

The head vigil is a tavern owner at one of the important crossroads in the Subura. Quintus Septimus is renowned as a man that gets things done for the people of the Subura. He is a tall man with a muscular body. A no-nonsense individual, he runs his area of the Subura like he runs his tavern. He has friends in the Senate and provides bodyguards for traveling senators on business of State. This morning sees Quintus counting his takings from the previous evening. He is well satisfied with the results. Sales are improving. Marius is absent and Sulla has brought his soldiers back from the east. There are plenty of patrons about. Quintus looks up from his counting. 'Ah, my good friend Demetrius, what brings you here? Who's looking after your shop today?' The men talk, while Quintus looks at Divina with a quizzical expression, and Demetrius then explains the youngster's role in the discovery of the dead girl. Quintus shakes his head, 'This dead girl may have dishonoured her father and has suffered the ultimate punishment,' he offers, believing this to be the most obvious motive. Now it's Demetrius's turn to disagree. 'Yes, Quintus, you may be right, but you should investigate the girl's circumstances. Nobody deserves to have their body dumped in an alley and left to become dog meat.' Quintus studies the child once more, then nods, 'Yes, yes, I'll have two of my men collect the body and I'll get a Greek physician friend of mine to look it over.' His attention is back on the child. 'You saw who put the body there?' The child nods and Quintus chalks down some details about a man and his horse and cart. Sometime later, the bundle is collected by two burly men. Davina is watching, from the tenement loft. She smiles to herself, happy that now the poor dead girl is being looked after.

Axateles made his living by treating the ailing populous of the Subura. The Greek physician, as expected, was not a wealthy man. But he was a free man; granted manumission by his last owner's will. He had also built up a notable clientele of the Equestrian order which, fortunately, did pay for his services and allowed him to live a moderate existence. Many years earlier, he had graduated from The Athenian Academy of Medicine and joined the Athenian Army as a surgeon. Unfortunately, he ended up taking sides with Mithridates and was captured by Roman soldiers, sold as a slave to a Roman merchant whose daughter was gravely ill. Axateles treated the daughter and saved her, thereby becoming a close friend with his master and family.

Axateles had seen a great deal of what men can inflict upon other men. But, today, as he looked down upon the young girl's body, he sighed. This, he considered, was a horrendous way for a young female to die. Clearly, she had been strangled, judging by the marks and bruising around her neck and there were traces of bleeding in her eyes, another symptom of asphyxiation. She had also been brutally raped with evident tears around her genitals and anus. Her blood loss would have killed her without the strangulation. Whoever was responsible certainly applied brute force. He wrote down some notes on a wax tablet and told his assistant to cover her up. He would have to speak to a praetor magistrate, probably Septimus, before she is buried. Who were her parents, he wondered?

'You know it's only serious matters that bring me through your door,' Axateles declared, squinting to read his wax tablet. 'Oh, and I thought today was going to be easy. I've had an easy morning, just squabbles and petty concerns. Anyway, what's so serious?' Septimua asked.

So Axateles related how he had a young lady lying dead on one of his slabs. She would be approximately fifteen years old. She has been brutally raped and sodomised. When the culprit or culprits finished with her, she was strangled. He went on to explain how a child had witnessed a man, with a horse and cart, had dumped the body outside an abandoned warehouse. The youngster claims to have seen this man with cart loads of vegetables leaving the city on the Via Appia several times recently.

'Oh dear, dear, a killing with malicious intent,' Septimus stated, shook his head, scowled, adding, 'We can certainly issue an indictment against this horse and cart merchant.' And then, Axateles declared, we'll get the youngster into the marketplace to identify the vegetable merchant. I'd better alert the vigils to be on standby for an arrest?

Septimus nodded, 'Yes, very well, but I have one major concern. We cannot have a child testifying in court against an adult, a magistrate would be reluctant to accept a child's testimony.'

'What if the vigils manage to get a confession?' Axateles asked. 'Now that is acceptable.' Septimus replied confidently, then added, have to inform you that the details of this case must be provided to Sulla. He must approve every capital case. All suspicious deaths or malicious killings are now being subject to government legislation. This is a good move on behalf of Sulla.'

Cassius became irritable with his Greek slave, Alexander. 'Will you get a move on?!' he shouted sternly, 'you're not like your namesake from Macedon!' he then exclaimed. Alexander tried to increase his pace but his breathing was laboured. He was some distance behind Cassius and thought, why did he pick me as a body guard? I can't even keep up with him. Cassius looked back. 'Good grief!' and shook his head.

They were making their way to The Field of Mars. Cassius was going to discuss his intention to defend Justinian in the military tribunal. He also wanted to counsel the youth on what questions he should and should not answer. Justinian had no presumption to the right of innocence until proven guilty. Republican justice did not work this way. He was considered guilty until he proved his innocence. The outcome would either be "absolvo" or "guilty".

Cassius waited by the entrance to the garrison, Alexander took ages to catch up. He was sweating and breathless, clearly fatigued by the long walk, Cassius scowled, obviously annoyed with the Greek but wouldn't rebuke him a second time. 'Now, you must wait here until I've completed my business inside the garrison. I have to talk with the guard's prefect, and the detained youth. It may take some time but don't get impatient and wander off. After I've finished, I need you to escort me home.' He looked at Alexander intently, 'You understand what I've just told you?' Alexander simply nodded, pointed to where he would take a seat and wait. Cassius, satisfied, turned and entered the prefect's tent.

A guard confronted Cassius, recognised the toga of a senator and saluted. Cassius responded with a nod and provided the soldier with an explanation of the nature of

Cassius's business. Satisfied, the soldier conducted him to the prefect's partition, a separate area of the tent detached for the prefect's privacy. Agrippa stood up and saluted the senator, motioned for him to take a seat with a heavy Greek table between them. Cassius related what his business was and how he'd also like to talk to Justinian. He was here to counsel and defend Justinian, he said. Whilst he was talking, Cassius couldn't help taking mental notes of Agrippa's facial expressions, clearly Agrippa wanted to speak. After allowing Cassius to finish his remarks, Agrippa smiled, 'The charges against the youth have changed to absent without permission, rather than desertion—as you must be aware, desertion is a very serious charge which could result in the death penalty carried out by his peers. As it stands now, the youth will face a defaulters' hearing and if found guilty, will receive either punishment duties or a fine and it will not result in a dishonourable discharge from the army.'

Cassius gave a sigh of relief, 'This is splendid news; does the youth know?' He asked anxiously. Agrippa stood up, 'Certainly, the youth gave me an explanation of what happened and I believed him. He had evidence of a sort. Perhaps you should talk to him now, he's billeted nearby. I'll provide a guard to escort you.'

Justinian heaved the bundle of firewood, tied together by hemp, and got it quickly to the entrance of his tent. He stacked it next to the brazier ready for the evening. The nights were becoming cooler. As a soldier under a disciplinary charge, he was expected to look after all the menial tasks such as washing pots and pans, attending the brazier, run errands for the other officer cadets to list a few. He bore no resentment;

this was how the army disciplined its soldiers, broke them down to become obedient servants of the republic. As a youngster, he appreciated the extra exercise.

Wiping his brow, he heard a familiar voice, 'Young man, I'm here to provide you with some legal advice.' Justinian swung around, 'Cassius, sir, it's such a blessing to see you,' he offered, a broad grin suffused his face. Cassius grabbed the youth's hand and shook it vigorously. 'Your mother spoke to me, told me about your problems of desertion and absence from your cohort!' Justinian was eager to interrupt but Cassius held his hand up to silence him. 'I know about the charge being downgraded to the lessor charge of being absent without permission but the Prefect Agrippa thinks you should strive for absolvo and have no blemish on your military record. After all, if you are going to become an officer, you need to have a clean slate.' Justinian kept nodding his head in agreement. 'Tell me, sir, how are any mother and sisters?' He asked, momentarily confusing Cassius. 'Uh, oh, yes, they're all under great strain but when I tell your mother about the new charge, she'll be greatly relieved,' he offered, adding, 'I'll go and see her as soon as I can.'

Lying in his bunk that evening, Justinian listened to his billet companions having discussions about their daily activities. He thought about his daily encounter with the senator. He had been told to answer questions truthfully, plead not guilty due to extenuating circumstances and, importantly, get these circumstances sorted out in his head. The prosecutor, whoever he is, will attempt to trip you, resulting in a guilty charge, Cassius offered. Not able to sleep, Justinian thought about Sabina, her tragically short life and the horrendous way she died. As he thought along these lines, he was determined he would get justice for the girl. Even if she did steal a pony, she shouldn't have been deprived of her life. The grain merchant was probably working the pony to death. At least Justinian had one good lead in the quest of finding the men: a grain merchant from somewhere near Formiae.

Aulus Rufmius chose the Via Cassia as his main route to Rome. Since disposing of the girl in the Subura, he had become very suspicious of his regular itinerary. He believed people stared at him, knowing what he had done. His simple job, to pick up and deliver vegetables to several villages south of Rome was becoming hazardous. Aulus now believed the gods considered him ill-favoured and were going to punish him. His body shook from worry; he whipped the old horse to go faster. 'Ye gods!' he offered to no one, realising he had never whipped the horse rope.

He was entering the Subura, tenements loomed large, alleys and nooks and crannies everywhere, again, people looking at him with accusatory stares. Even the children were pointing fingers at him. He lowered his head, attempted to get the old horse to lift its pace.

Aulus's body shook involuntary, up ahead, four men were blocking the road. 'Oh Jupiter, help me,' he pleaded. He noticed the four strangers were carrying batons attached to their hips by a red sash. Vigils, Aulus suddenly realised, and they were walking towards his horse. One of them grabbed the horse's rope, preventing the horse from advancing. Aulus scowled, 'Hey, get away from my horse!' he shouted. The men ignored him and approached his cart. Two men reached up and grabbed Aulus, pulling him off the seat. He landed on the ground with a thump and was quickly hauled up onto his feet. 'We need to talk to you, merchant. You're coming with us. We'll look after your horse and cart, get a move on, this way.'

Altogether, there were four soldiers for the defaulter's session. They all stood at attention, awaiting the summons to enter the partition of the command tent, set aside for petty trials. The first soldier was summoned and was quickly marched into the partition. After a short period of time shouting was heard from inside; it sounded like the prosecuting officer; someone was whimpering and begging for leniency. Justinian took a deep breath, tried to get a handle on his composure. A sentence was handed down in the chamber, sounded like the defaulter was being demoted and ordered to muck out stables for a month.

Suddenly, two officers entered the command tent, marched straight into the trial chamber. A lengthy conversation took place; the two officers plus two guards exited the chamber and marched over to Justinian. One of the officers, Agrippa, avoiding eye contact with the youth, declared, 'Cadet Justinian Cornelius, it has been attested that you were involved in the rape and murder of a young girl, named Sabina. I hereby arrest you and will hold you in detention until such time as a trial can be arranged.' Justinian's mouth fell open, but he was speechless and could only mutter inanities, not making much sense. Agrippa ordered the guards to shackle the youth, remove him to the detention wing. Manacled, Justinian was marched to the prefect's headquarters.

He stood; eyes wide open, staring at his cell: a huge box affair on wheels with small vents in each of the four sides. It was transport designed to convey prisoners from one place to another, and it was dreadful. Justinian was led up the steps and pushed through the doorway, ending up slumped on the rough wooden floor. The door slammed shut and a padlock was secured to the latch. Inside, it was dark and gloomy; there was a distinct odour of urine, excrement and vomit. Justinian gagged several times but managed to stifle his spasms and, finally, sat quietly. Outside, he heard familiar noises, soldiers practicing drills, centurions screaming orders, someone practicing on a horn, wood-chopping, all familiar sounds of an army camp. He desperately wanted to speak to Agrippa, but knew he'd have to wait.

Agrippa stood in the rear entrance to the guard tent, staring at the wheeled transporter. He felt for the youth, and sincerely believed he was innocent. Justinian was not a rapist, killer, but he'd been swept-up in a tempest of turmoil, all because he'd befriended a girl with a stolen pony. Rape and murder, the men responsible should be flogged and exiled at the very least. He stamped his foot in frustration; surely there was something he could do to help the youth. He sighed, he understood he was putting his army career at risk but he felt the need to help the youth, round-up the culprits and bring them to trial immediately, Agrippa began formulating a plan.

Catalina had friends and clients everywhere. He didn't welcome the news about Justinian, but he could use it to his advantage. After all, despite how unsophisticated Julia was, she still loved her brother. Yes, he considered, he being a senator, could pull some strings and, the prize, Julia's heart. Catalina was born of an aristocratic dynasty, the desire to devise was innate, and he was a controller and manipulator of people who mattered. *Dignitas*, to Catalina, meant the very survival of his own kind, the founding fathers of Rome, all the way back to Romulus, then the early kings and, the senatorial succession. In Catalina's mind, the threat to Rome's survival, known as the "*Novus Homoines*", the new men, such as Cicero and Marius, who belonged to the new tier of society, the Equestrian order, merchants, bankers, land owners, horse and livestock owners. Catalina believed he was Fortuna's favourite, destined to establish and uphold the old senatorial order.

Catalina had begun his quest, recruiting loyalist members of the aristocracy. He needed as many as possible and Julia belonged to the Cornelia dynasty, her family must be included. But now, her brother is accused of raping and murdering a young woman. Julia believed he was innocent, therefore Catalina believed he was innocent. Something must be done to get Justinian out of guard prison—he was a definite recruit for the Roman revolution. So, Catalina began doing what he did best, devising.

Justinian had been in the lock-up for twenty-four hours and had one meagre meal. Having had very little sleep, he felt exhausted and, had difficulty in getting his body to follow orders. He attempted to lift himself off the floor and, perhaps, reach one of the vents and suck in some air. Owing to the narrowness of the transporter, Justinian placed his feet on the opposite wall and squared his back on the wall behind him, then applied pressure attempting to slide up the wall. After a strenuous effort, he got high enough to let his feet support his weight, but he had to stoop, owing to is height. He commenced, taking in lungful of air, and suddenly, felt dizzy from his efforts. He rested and took advantage of a soft breeze coming through the vent.

'How can we help you, senator?' Agrippa asked the young city official. Catalina, with his ice-cold eyes, studied the prefect for a few moments, then spoke, 'I've come to see the young soldier who is being charged with malicious killing. His family belong to one of my clients, and, the youngster is a Roman citizen with citizen's rights.'

Agrippa knew all this but he an uneasy sense about this young senator. 'Certainly, you may see him. I'll get a guard to escort you to his place of confinement.' The guard finally arrived and led Catalina through the back entrance towards the transporter wagon. 'Ye gods, you've put the youth in that?' Catalina angrily asked.

'It was authorised by Sulla,' the guard replied.

'But why the box-cart?' Catalina queried.

'He's being transported to Capua to be tried by Sulla,'

'Holy Jupiter!' Catalina exclaimed, adding, 'Why's Sulla so interested in the trial of a youth?'

'Here, why all the questions, senator? Surely you know about Sulla and his criminal courts' reforms?'

'Uh, yes, you're right; I've heard several speeches about the reforms. Thank you, guard, we had better be off and talk to the detainee,' Catalina offered.

Justinian could hear a conversation but not what was being said. Trying to look through the vent was awkward, but then, suddenly, a voice from the other side of the door. 'Justinian, can you hear me?' Catalina asked. 'Who is it?' Justinian responded.

'Senator Catalina,' his voice dropped to a whisper, 'your family, they're devastated about your new charges. What the hell happened?'

Justinian scowled, 'What's all this got to do with you, senator?' he spat back.

'I'm here to help you, Justinian; you're going to need all the help you can get, young man. You can drop the animosity and be thankful you have some senators wanting to help you,' Catalina sternly declared.

Justinian sighed, 'Yes, you're correct. I do need help, sorry. Please tell my mother and sisters I'm innocent, and I love them.' A wave of exhaustion hit him again. 'How are you going to help me?'

Catalina moved into the door; spoke softly, 'When you speak to me, whisper. But first, listen to what I have to say. Tomorrow you will be transported to Capua. Justinian almost shouted 'Capua!'

'Sshh!' Catalina interrupted, 'Will you keep your voice down, please?'

'Sorry,' the youth offered. Catalina continued, 'Apparently Sulla has taken an interest in your case. He wants to supervise your trial. You will be leaving here at sunrise, travelling on the Via Appian.' Catalina looked around, nobody present. 'Some of my men are going to hold up the guards and free you from the transporter. I promise you, nobody will get hurt. Once you're free, you must head for and locate those men responsible for the girl's death. Some of my men will help you locate these men. I have a number of clients in Formiae ready and willing. 'Incredulous,' Justinian opened his mouth to protest but Catalina ordered him to be silent. 'Listen! How do you expect to get away with this crime?

Sulla's looking for a show piece, he wants to impress with his new reforms. Where do you think that leaves you?'

Justinian bit his lower lip, he once thought he may have had a chance, but now he felt desperate. 'What do I do once you've got me free?' He asked, legs beginning to tremble.

'You will join my revolt. I've recruited hundreds of people from the Picentes, Samnites to the Lucani. They're all waiting for the appropriate time. But time is not right, not while Sulla is dictator with military powers.

'What about the men who killed the girl?' Justinian demanded.

'All in good time, young man, first things first, we have to get you freed.' Catalina replied confidently.

Agrippa watched Catalina from the guard tent's rear entrance. Catalina had been talking to the youth for quite some time. Agrippa knew about Catalina's reputation. He represented that aspect of the Senate which left a bad taste in the mouths of the lower classes of Roman society; rich, privileged, ill-natured, untrustworthy and powerful. Agrippa sighed. What was he up to? He asked himself. Why did the likes of him have an interest in the youth? What good can come out of this?

Attia didn't know what to think. Cassius had told her that her son would probably face a lesser, petty charge and he would be freed. She felt elated. Later, Catalina conveyed the news that it was alleged that Justinian had committed rape and murder and would likely receive a severe sentence, possibly death penalty. This was dreadful news. She felt numb, her body and mind felt alien, this couldn't be happening to her. She kept seeing Julia's face and she was trying to tell her something but it didn't register, she couldn't comprehend. All she understood was if it was true, and her son is found guilty, she would lose everything, her home, her possessions and the investments her late husband made. To further unsettle her mind, Cassius, the other senator, had tried to seduce her during his last visit two days ago. He had been clumsy in his efforts—she had blocked his attempts to kiss and fondle her. Though she had sensed the pleasure of his touch, she fought back the tempting desires in her own body. After all, she had just started her period of mourning for her husband. Julia broke into her thoughts, 'Mamma, try and lie down, get some sleep. There's nothing we can do for Justinian, let Cassius and Catalina do what they can. I know my brother is innocent and the truth will shine through in the end.'

'I do hope you are right, Julia,' Attia pleaded as she eased herself down on her bed. 'Now let momma sleep, Julia.' Wake me if there's any news.'

And there was news, further bad news, Catalina returned to Attia's villa and informed her that her son was being transported to Capua for his trial under the supervision of Sulla as part of his crime reforms. Inconsolable, she once again, fled to her bed chamber. Catalina set his eyes on Julia's enticing body but Julia wasn't in the mood, so, he then set his sights on the bookish Antonia; she just wanted to discuss the terrible mistake Rome made in totally destroying Carthage sixty years ago. Catalina shook his head, then retreated to the atrium and thought about his plan for tomorrow.

Justinian sat against the transporter wall; his mind plagued with concerns. Could Catalina's outrageous plan actually work? What was his motive for risking his neck? What if the plan failed, what then? Justinian scowled, wishing he could speak with Agrippa. And, another thing, if he got out of the transporter, escaped, he'd now be an escaped felon, a true rebel.

The new dawning meant different things for different people. Justinian awoke with a jolt; his wagon-transporter was being hitched to a pair of horses. Soldiers' voices issuing orders and directions could be heard around the transporter. Before long, the transporter jerked forward, escorted by four cavalry officers as guards. Justinian got to his feet and stared through one of the small vents. He counted the four cavalrymen detailed for the journey to Capua, the most senior being a Tessararius (Senior Sergeant). This task is simple enough, travel to Capua, about a full day and night journey, then hand the prisoner over to the Capuan Guard sometime tomorrow, then return to Rome. The four cavalrymen should be back in barracks in two or three days. By rights, sometime in the next week or so Justinian is going to be face to face with the great man, Sulla.

Justinian had never been to another city outside Rome. As the transporter groaned from the woodwork and the iron-rimmed wheels clanked and squealed along the cobble-stone road, Justinian, eager, studied the landscape of crops, vineyards and roadside inns. For the countryside, it was well populated and people were busy outdoors with various chores. The countryside here was vastly different from the trip he once made south to Antium. The Via Appia was surrounded by dense forests. Here, the landscape was captivating, productive and made you feel proud to be a citizen of the greatest city in the known world. But these thoughts only made Justinian sullen and, using his back, slid down to slump on the floor. The patriotic sensitivities quickly ended.

A full afternoon of the journey later, the transporter came to an abrupt halt with the groan of brakes. It jolted Justinian out of his lethargy. He heard raised voices, but not Catalina's. It was impossible for Justinian to witness the events taking place but six horsemen had surrounded the transporter, four men held bows with arrows aimed at the Roman guards. The attackers had the clear advantage, short swords, clearly useless with archers at the ready. One man, with a gruff voice, demanded the door be opened and the youth freed. The guard holding the reins complied, realising that he could be badly wounded if he refused the attackers.

Justinian slowly stepped out of the transporter into fresh air. For a few moments, he felt dizzy and leaned against the wooden frame of the doorway. The man with the commanding voice told the youth to mount one of the horses, double-up behind one of the archers. Justinian walked towards one of the archers. At this moment things suddenly turned chaotic. Another voice with authoritativeness filled the air. 'You men drop your bows and arrows or you will be gutted by arrows of the Roman army.' Justinian counted at least fifteen cavalry officers, all with bows extended and arrows aimed. The men rose from the ditches on either side of the roadway. Justinian, feeling unsafe, slipped back into the prison transporter and closed the door. One of the original abductors dismounted and strode over to Agrippa and shook his hand. 'This is only a few of them, sir. Catalina has raised a small army; they're all over the mainland. However, it's too early for a revolt. Catalina is not ready, he needs more men.' Agrippa nodded, 'You've done a good job, soldier. By the time we start working on these rogues, I'm sure we'll get plenty of intelligence to infiltrate the other groups.' They walked over to the transporter and summoned Justinian.

With the original horsemen bound together, Agrippa addressed Justinian. 'I'm glad you spoke to me last night about this plot. I'm sure Sulla will view you favourably for the trial. I've suspected Senator Catalina for some time. He's a crafty sod. Now, we need to apprehend those culprits who killed the girl.'

Justinian, nodded his head in agreement, 'Sir, I'm so thankful that we talked last night. I was beginning to despair of ever seeing you again. At the moment you and Cassius are my true friends and the only support I've got.'

'I think we accomplished quite a bit with this haul,' Agrippa declared, adding, 'We are a long way north of where your enemies are. I think we must make a start. We have horses on this farm behind us. Let's get three of them and make a start for Antium.'

The three horses, two riders and a pack horse with supplies soon got onto the road, heading south. They kept the horses at an easy pace, chatting about a strategy for finding the three men. With the following information already at hand: the owner of the pony was a flour merchant who provides for the villages west of Formiae. He hired two ex-gladiators, tough fellows for protection and labour; one of these fellows had a nasty gash on one of his cheeks from chasing Sabina; both of these men were heavily scarred due to their past professions, lastly; the boss man's horse had a chestnut tinted coat. Agrippa was reasonably pleased with this information. 'I think these fellows will be easy to find. When we strike the right area, the locals should be able to tell us their location.'

'Sir, there's one thing that concerns me about all this,' Justinian remarked, with a scowl, 'The three of them could accuse me of being the killer—that's three against one, as far as allegations go, a prosecutor could make an easy case of it.'

'Yes, I've thought about this problem and I think the vegetable merchant could be an asset for defence. And the other thing is: there's no motive for your involvement; why would you stick with the girl right to the end. A killer would not have done this,' Agrippa surmised.

'Yes, I just wanted to make sure her remains were looked after.'

Catalina's mood just got worse; his gang of ruffians had been apprehended; one of them had been an agent working for the military. 'Hope those fools can keep me out of it' he said abruptly, before Julia opened her mouth. 'You're the fool, Catalina,' she offered, her face a mask of disdain. She wondered why she liked this man so much. There would never be any future for them as a couple; he was too volatile, both politically and sexually. 'Fancy believing you could beguile the army,' she spat, angrily.

'I only tried to free your brother, get him out of that wooden monstrosity,' he replied, hoping to dispel her anger. 'It didn't work,' Julia replied, looking at him intently, 'No, that's not it; you've got an ulterior motive. Those men will probably be thrown off the Tarpeion Rock for their efforts.'

'It's not my fault they had an informer in their ranks,' he argued. Unexpectedly, the softly spoken Antonia interrupted their conversation, 'Catalina, you are going to be famous one day,' the pair quickly swung around to confront Antonia, she added, 'But for all the wrong reasons.' Catalina and Julia, in unison, hollered, 'Oh shut up, Antonia!'

Back on the Via Appia, heading south, Agrippa and Justinian kept their horses at a steady trot. Justinian was not a proficient horseman, his experience with horses was rudimentary and now that he'd been in the saddle for the whole afternoon, his inner thighs and backside were painfully chafing. Agrippa sensed the youth's discomfort and suggested they walk the horses until dusk. They settled on a place to camp overnight. Justinian recognised the area where he met Marius's bodyguard, where he also lost his sword and helmet. This reminded him of the tunic he was wearing when he waded into the stream to wash himself and his tunic. Agrippa set-up a four-man tent and set about preparing a meal.

Wrapped in a man's shawl, Justinian joined Agrippa for a meal of boiled rice and honey. 'This is very good, sir. It's so simple and tasty.' Justinian remarked, licking his lips.

'It's what we have on long marches, a no-fuss meal that keeps you going,' Agrippa explained. He put down his bowl, wiped his mouth. 'We've got to develop a strategy for catching these men, there are only two of us and three of them, two of them are ex-gladiators, they'll be strong, so once we locate them, I'll report to the nearest garrison and get some assistance. It'll appear more officious if there's a detail of guards, less resistance hopefully,' adding with a frown, 'that's the simple approach. However, these things are always more complex in reality, there may be more men on the farm, they may have a cache of weapons, and they certainly have horses,' he declared.

After dusk, and tending to the horses, they prepared their bedding in the tent. Both lay there, ruminating on what may or may not happen on the morrow. Justinian thought about Agrippa. How would he ever be able thank this man for having such faith in me? Agrippa, he considered, epitomised the army's recipe for success. The officer class was the backbone of the army, and that's why Rome was such a mighty city, its influence spreading far and wide. Justinian felt proud to be a trainee officer, but first, he needed to clear his name of any misdeeds. It wasn't long before both fell into a deep sleep.

Both were up at dawn, Justinian used a special balm for his chafing. After having more rice and honey for breakfast, both resumed their journey towards Formiae. With the township about quarter of a day's trot, they kept their vision on the passing countryside, mostly small landholdings. One or two men were working the small crops, mainly carrots, tomatoes and beetroot. Justinian began to sense some confusion in his perception of merchants and vegetable distribution. He turned to Agrippa. 'The man who had the horse and cart, why did he have to go to Rome to purchase vegetables and come back up here to sell his wagon load?' Agrippa looked at the youth, offered, 'Because of syndicates, all vegetables are harvested by the farmers, and then shipped to Rome. Why? Because they are guaranteed a better price in Rome. If all the landholders agree to do this, then they'll make more money. If they decide to sell locally, they'll make less money and it won't be worth looking after a crop of whatever if you add all the money invested in a crop planting, labour, water, haulage and sales. These syndicates are supposedly run by the government, but are usually run by unscrupulous dealers out for a profit, guaranteeing the government a cut. Everybody is happy except the landholder. You understand?'

Justinian nodded, 'Yes, to a degree, it just seems there's lots of wasted time—travelling to Rome and bringing the load back here,' he replied with a frown.

'It's a system that seems to work, it leads to competitiveness between landowners. The downside is the more a vegetable floods the market, the lower the price. So, in a sense, the system is self-regulating.' The youth listened carefully and tried to sort things out in his mind. He knew that after completing twenty-five years in the army, he could be retired to a block of farmland somewhere, where hundreds of retired soldiers were scraping a living off farmland.

As they got closer to Formiae they came across an inn with stables. The horses were handed over, the pair organised accommodation for the night and arranged refreshing baths. Scrubbed and invigorated, they made themselves comfortable in the tavern with some watered wine. At first, only a few locals visited the tavern. The pair, inconspicuously, listened to the conversations between the locals which mainly centred on Sulla's proscriptions and prices of produce. Justinian, after several wines, found himself starting to fall asleep, until his ears caught a conversation going on between two locals: 'Gordianus is complaining about grain prices again, saying it's not worth his labour to grind flour—the government's robbing him blind, he says…' Justinian looked to Agrippa, but he was nodding, listening to the same conversation. 'Gordianus,' Justinian whispered, 'should we make inquiries?'

'You stay here, listen for anything important, ask the tavern keeper if he knows this chap, Gordianus' Agrippa replied, and got up to talk to the tavern keeper. Agrippa managed to speak to the tavern-keeper for quite a while. Justinian didn't gain any more important information from the two locals. When Agrippa returned, sat down, he offered, 'This Gordianus is a grain merchant, not too far from here, he has a number of men in his employ, mainly deserters from the army. I also asked about any missing young females from around these parts, couldn't help me on that one.'

'Nothing more of interest between our two friends here,' Justinian said. 'Pity, let's get something to eat and have an early night,' Agrippa suggested, stifling a yawn.

Chapter 6

Formiae, a coastal township of possibly three thousand souls; for Romans, Formiae is a kind of resort with many of the dwellings unoccupied during the colder months. However, the current mild weather ensured a throng of Romans escaping Rome's high humidity. Approaching from the north on the Via Appia, traffic is heavy: horse-drawn carts, litters and pedestrians provided a slow trudge into the township for the pair and their packhorse.

Agrippa, ever the strategist, decided the first visit should be to the local tax collector's' office, in the municipal chambers. The plan was to locate Sabina's mother, or guardian, and impart the sad news about her daughter. Agrippa and Justinian were in military uniforms which, hopefully, would provide them a degree of officialdom. Agrippa, being a junior tribune of the soldiers, would profess the required authority. They were met by an assistant to the legate who listened to Agrippa's explanation of the girl's death, her single name, or *nomen*, instead of *tria-nomina* the fact she lived with her mother who was a sole parent. The pair were well known in inns and taverns because they entertained by dancing and singing and, no doubt, in other entertaining pastimes.

The official brought out some registry scrolls; names, births and whether or not they owed taxes. It was understood by all that 'entertainers' did not pay taxes. However, the young girl should have been listed under 'births' along with her mother and father. And, Sabina was found, with her mother listed but "father unknown". Sabina would have been fourteen this year, which surprised Justinian, he thought she was older.

The mother and daughter had resided on a small farm on the outskirts of Formiae. Directions were supplied to Agrippa, whilst the official duly noted the girl's death by malicious killing. When the pair finally found the property, it wasn't a farm, it was a small holding with a dilapidated hovel for a dwelling. A few chickens pecked the earth for morsels of food. The pair carefully approached what looked to be a front door, knocked, and after a short period, a soft voice responded, 'Yes. Who is it?' Agrippa answered, 'Good morning, madam, I'm junior tribune, Agrippa; I'm here to give you information about your daughter, Sabina.'

Immediately, from behind the door, a noise erupted, items were being pushed over—the mother was hastily clearing a passage to the door. She was wailing, 'Sabina, oh my sweet Sabina, oh, oh.'

Agrippa cast a quick glance to Justinian, who frowned; this wasn't going to be easy. The door creaked open to reveal a middle-aged woman, stooped and crippled by hardship and undernourishment. With hair thinning and dominant cheekbones and pale skin, she could have been over fifty but probably only thirty-five. She blinked from the sudden light. 'Have you seen my Sabina, have you brought her home?' She stammered, her appeal was urgent and heartfelt.

‘I’m so sorry, ma’am, but, uh, the news about Sabina is not good’ Agrippa offered, attempting to sound as sincere as possible. The woman raised her hand to cover her mouth, Agrippa continued, ‘Sabina was maliciously killed by a group of men near Rome. Her body has been interred in a plot for homeless souls. I’m so sorry to have to bear this news to you.’

The mother whimpered behind the hand over her mouth. Justinian moved forward to put his arm around her shoulders and lead her to a seat. The single room was small with minimal furniture: two wicker armchairs, a double bed-base and a table. Scattered around the room were the simple possessions of an impoverished soul: loose garments, worn sandals, threadbare blankets and assorted cheap trinkets. Justinian did see a small bust of Tiberius Gracchus. He had her sit in an armchair. Agrippa removed his helmet, ‘this is Justinian, he befriended Sabina, knows the men who killed her. We’re here to apprehend those men and, hopefully, have them punished.’

Justinian, standing next to the mother, asked, ‘Do you know anything about a pony? When I met Sabina, she was leading a pony, looking for somewhere to have the creature stabled and cared for.’

The mother, sobbing, started to regain her composure. ‘She loved that pony, talked about it all the time. It belonged to a merchant hereabouts; he was cruel to the animal. Sabina said she would get the animal and find it a better home.’ She fell forward and wailed again. Justinian pulled her back up into the armchair. Sobbing, she said, ‘I knew this would end up in misfortune, she wouldn’t listen to me, oh gods!’

The pair remained with the mother until midday, found out where the pony was worked and the man who worked it, Gordanius. They promised the mother they would return once the men were apprehended, convicted and, compensated her for her lost child. Both felt quite depressed after the ordeal, they wished that there were some forms of social welfare for needy people like Sabina's mother. Ordinarily, villagers, for instance, helped each other in times of tribulation. However, Sabina's mother was isolated and had become something of a recluse and lived on scraps. She needed help, and Agrippa decided he would find her help. He needed to also find a good lawyer back in Rome. The likes of Cicero and Cato came to mind.

Riding back to Formiae, the pair agreed to visit the garrison. Ideally, they should recruit a guard of about eight soldiers for their visit to Gordanius, who had about six thugs of his own. In military terms, Formiae was a modest Latium town, didn't pose a threat to Rome during the Social War and, therefore, didn't warrant a large contingent of soldiers. In charge of the small garrison of thirty-five soldiers was a junior tribune, an inferior rank to Prefect Agrippa. However, Agrippa had no signed authority to recruit soldiers for the apprehension of civilians. Agrippa was going to have to bluff his way around the Junior Tribune, Gneus Annius. The junior tribune was a stickler for protocol, which included respect for rank. He smartly saluted Agrippa and offered him the best seat in his tiny office. The two officers began the process of negotiating. After a short period, Agrippa left the office with a wry grin on his face.

Chapter 7

Agrippa could borrow six garrison soldiers for the apprehension of the culprits. The junior tribune suspected Agrippa of being embroiled in some misdeed but didn't ask, and overlooked the mischief. For all he knew, Agrippa might be apprehending Marius or Marius Junior, a worthy, though secretive, mission. Though, he did wonder why he hadn't brought his own soldiers; the other troop looking for Marius a few days ago had enough men.

Of Gaius Marius, news began to filter into Rome that the great man had died. Many hated Marius for his manic savagery brought on by mental illness and hatred of Sulla; Axateles, the physician had called it an 'aberration' brought about by a stroke. It was only a matter of thirty years ago when Marius and his army defeated the Germanic tribes threatening Rome from the north, the Cimbri and the Teutoni. Previously, Marius had re-organised the army, introduced more efficient weapons, had been elected consul six times and was considered "first man in Rome" by a unanimous Senate. And, today, even his son, Marius Junior, is proscribed for death by Sulla.

With six soldiers in tow, Agrippa and Justinian set their sights on the property of grain merchant Gordanius. Away from the coast, they travelled inland, estimating half a day's journey. All the soldiers were on horseback with two pack horses in tow. The further inland they got from the coast, the more gentle the terrain. Among the soldiers was one centurion, a twenty-year veteran, a no-nonsense, baffle-hardened individual called Lucius Sicca. He kept the other soldiers in tight formation, having their respect and trust. Agrippa was well pleased with the selection of men under his command. As a unit, he knew they would do their best.

By midday, they had the property in their sights, Agrippa conferred with Centurion Sicca; both agreeing that the sensible approach would be to reconnoitre the property and try to work out how many men were in Gordianus's employ. A track ran parallel to the property, so Agrippa and Sicca had the remaining soldiers and Justinian demount, tether the horses and spread out so they could observe what activities were taking place and how many men could be observed. They spotted the pony, slowly driving the grinding stone, and there were three men filling bags of flour creating a dust cloud that would be advantageous to the soldiers. Asked if he could identify Gordanius, Justinian said no. The main gate was opened and Agrippa, accompanied by Sicca, went through. Whilst trotting towards the main building, Agrippa informed the Centurion how he'd like to deal with the situation. They approached the three men loading the flour. The men ceased their activity and stared at the two soldiers who remained mounted. 'Good afternoon, we're here to talk to the owner,

Gordanius. Is he hereabouts?' Agrippa asked in a conciliatory tone.

'Aye, he's doing the accounts,' one of the men answered.

'Could you fetch him, please,' Agrippa requested, with a more serious note.

'I'll get him,' another man piped up, and turned towards the building. Agrippa quickly noticed the scarred cheek of this man's face. The fellow entered the building and some time elapsed before the merchant emerged, muttering and complaining, 'What's the meaning of this intrusion? Can't you see that I've a business to run? What do you want?'

'Sir, did you have a pony go missing about a month ago? I believe a young lady was responsible for the theft of the animal, is that correct?' The owner took some time to reply, clearly trying to decide whether or not he should implicate himself. 'Aye, that's right, but I got the animal back and, uh, gave her a piece of my mind. I let her go, she's a poor un, lives with her mother,' he offered.

'Am I to take it, you didn't punish the girl?'

'As I said, I let her go. There was a young soldier with her. Is there a problem?' He asked, with a frown.

'The girl was raped and maliciously killed.' Agrippa declared, dropping his conciliatory facade. The merchant was beginning to protest his innocence when Agrippa added, 'She was dealt with quite brutally.'

'We left her safe and sound; she was with some young soldier. I could identify him. He looked like a shifty character. I believe he was on the run from the army.'

'That young soldier in question is here today, just over there.' Agrippa swung around in the saddle and waved to the group of soldiers waiting on the outskirts of the property. The six mounted soldiers moved as one, towards the building.

A look of panic swept over the merchant's face, 'Here, you can't just come onto my private property and start throwing accusations at us. I tell you, that bleeding' youngster must have been responsible for the girl's death,' he shouted at Agrippa. Lucius squirmed in the saddle, 'Look out, sir, there's more of them.' Three more men emerged from the building, carrying wooden pikes. Agrippa shook his head; he didn't want this to happen. 'I must warn you, sir, we will retaliate if anyone attempts to threaten any of my soldiers,' he declared loudly. The six horse soldiers pulled up, a cloud of dust engulfing Agrippa and Lucius. One of the merchant's men swung his pike and knocked a soldier off his horse. The soldier hit the ground with a sickening thud, all short swords were quickly drawn; horses began moving in different directions. A soldier hit a man over the head with his sword pommel, the man dropped with a groan, blood streaming down his face. Agrippa's horse bucked, he remained in the saddle. 'Everybody, cease fighting at once!' Agrippa bellowed. Men and horses began backing away, eyeing each other warily. Justinian too, tightening the reins, tugged his horse's head sideways to get him clear of the melee. He thought he was clear but, without warning, a rock struck his shoulder and Justinian dropped like a sack of flour to the ground. Lying there, moaning, Justinian watched as Agrippa finally got things under control. The final tally of wounded men was equal: two of the flour merchant's men were down, and two soldiers.

The soldiers had Gordanius under arrest. He was escorted back to Formiae garrison. Once there, he was locked in a cell.

Agrippa had no authority to arrest this man but he needed to get him to Rome as soon as possible. The Republican Senate had no statutes for murder. If these crimes didn't affect the running of the government, then the authorities didn't concern themselves. However, if someone had a strong suspicion that a person was guilty of a malicious killing then they could appeal to the elected praetor, or a magistrate, and have the person judged before a jury of elected officials. A defence lawyer and a prosecutor would be appointed to handle the case. The case against Gordanius was flimsy, only one witness, Justinian, and, he did not witness the actual malicious killing. Gordanius was seeking an absolvo and alleging that Justinian was the actual murderer. There were three witnesses stacked against the youth.

As if Justinian didn't have enough to worry about, he also had a dislocated shoulder from the fall and needed to see a physician as soon as possible. The pain throughout his right shoulder and arm was unbearable, and the sling didn't help. He was given directions to a Greek medico called Praxateles, who also served as an army surgeon. A softly spoken, middle-aged man of diminutive stature, he possessed the most delicate fingers that Justinian ever saw on a man. 'Ah, my good fellow, you've popped the arm bone head out of its shoulder socket, we must get it back in before it causes more damage. How are you feeling?' He asked. Justinian was about to reply, when the physician added, 'Stupid question, it's very painful I know. Now let's get you onto this couch. I'll get you some oil of poppies to dull the pain while I pop it back in.' He made sure the youth was comfortable, removed the sling while Justinian "Ooohed" and "Aaahed". He made sure the youth's arm was straight, by his side, then went over to a cabinet and removed a vial. 'Here' he said, 'swallow this in one gulp, quickly now.' Justinian quickly swallowed the draft, made a face, 'Yuuck! That's bloody awful!' He sat back down on the couch and shook his head. 'Ye gods, no more of that stuff, I beg you!' Suddenly, Justinian felt his eye lids getting heavy. He tried to keep them open, but was engulfed by blackness.

'You can wake up now soldier.' The voice uttered it again, 'You can wake up now soldier.' Justinian stirred, opened his eyes, 'Whaa,' he managed. 'Your shoulder and arm have been set to rights, you can go back to the garrison now,' Praxateles explained. Justinian shook his head, attempting to comprehend what the physician was telling him. Fifteen minutes later, Justinian was making his way to the military depot with his arm in a sling. He greeted Agrippa with a semblance of a smile on his face, so relieved to be free of pain. 'You've a visitor in the tavern, his name's Cicero, he's having a meal with the prefect. Mind your manners now.'

Not a handsome man, but certainly a man of distinction and polish, his senatorial toga was spotless and immaculately creased. This was one of the most celebrated law-makers in Rome. Justinian slowly made his way over to the table. Both men looked up as the youth got closer to the table. 'Good afternoon, sir, I'm Justinian Cornelia, I'm accused of rape and malicious killing…' Cicero put up his hand, bringing Justinian to surcease his talking. 'My good man, could you be quiet while I'm finishing off my dinner. I'll be with you directly,' he declared, while slurping the contents off his spoon. The garrison prefect finished his meal and dismissed himself. Cicero told Justinian to sit. The great legal mind sipped some watered wine, sat back in his chair and looked at the youth. 'So, you're being tried for rape and malicious killing. You don't strike me as a killer, or a rapist for that matter,' Justinian began to protest his innocence, but Cicero waved his finger, 'I don't want to hear whether or not your innocent, I'm an advocate and I will be conducting your defence, so it's up to me to have the allegations disproved. How many witnesses are claiming you murdered this girl?' He asked while wiping his mouth.

'Four,' Justinian anxiously replied, adding, 'but I didn't do it, I…' Again, Cicero waved his finger, 'did you not hear what I just said about your guilt or not?' Chiding the youth.

'Yes, but…' Cicero banged the table with his hand. Justinian flinched, sat back, 'Yes, I won't say anything.'

'Good, now listen to me. Sulla is in Capua devising reforms for the thirty criminal courts. He's looking into the question of murder becoming judged as a capital crime, punishable by death. He's very interested in your case. Sulla is not an easy man to deal with, he's no diplomat and he's by no means conciliatory in his dealings with lawyers. I've not only got to deal with four witnesses making allegations against you,, but I've got to deal with someone who thinks he's the supreme law maker in Rome and doesn't like being misguided, or thwarted in his decision making and conclusions. He already thinks you are guilty.' Cicero hesitated, scowled, continued, 'You understand what I'm up against, son?' Yes, I know exactly what you're up against, Justinian thought. You are more concerned about your own skin than you are mine. This man is ambitious. Ye gods, what a mess.

Chapter 8

Justinian recalled the occasions when he listened to Cicero making speeches in the Senate house. As a young man, Marcus Tullius Cicero was an exceptional orator and most of the listening senators were greatly influenced by this *novus homo* from Arpinum. He was admirable, his perorations superb. For Cicero, elocution and delivery were an important element in his powers of persuasion. Justinian, however, knew that Cicero had enemies owing to his status. As Cicero grew in stature, he would become a great man in the Republic but he would die at the hands of a greater man. Of course, Justinian didn't know this, and, for the moment, he felt a sense of relief that this man would defend him in court.

Justinian's trial was set for a month's time. The fact that Sulla took an interest in the case, and had already made a judgement was worrying. As he made his way to the garrison, he spotted his sisters coming in the opposite direction. Julia was first to see him, she grabbed Antonia and, together, they raced to meet him. Their exuberance surprised him, both kissed and hugged him. 'Jupiter! What's all this for?' He cried out, excitedly. Julia, taking his arm, said, 'Oh, brother, we've been so worried about you since Catalina tried to free you!' Justinian scowled, exclaimed, 'The man's a blockhead!' Both sisters nodded enthusiastically, 'Yes, we know brother. Cassius has hired someone to keep an eye on him.'

The trio made their way back towards the Field of Mars and Justinian tried to explain the sling. Julia shook her head. 'Don't you want to see momma, she's so downcast?' She asked.

'Of course I do,' he almost shouted, but squeezed her arm, 'I'm sorry but I cannot, for I'm still under detention. Agrippa allowed me to visit the army surgeon and I had to visit Cicero about my case.'

'Is he your advocate?' Antonia eagerly asked; her eyes wide. 'Yes, he is, but I'm not sure I like him.' Antonia stopped walking, 'What!' She almost screamed, 'Are you serious?' Before he could answer, Antonia added, shouted, 'He's the greatest advocate in Rome' and that, settled his concerns about Cicero.

Chapter 9

The month dragged by. Some people were busy, the advocate and the prosecutor spent time meeting and talking to people connected to the case. A praetor magistrate was appointed to oversee the court's progress and ensure the cases were impartially conducted. Citizens were selected for jury service. Sulla returned to Rome, proscriptions recommenced and Catalina secured himself a new occupation, which proved quite lucrative; he joined the official groups involved in the confiscation of the property of the proscribed. Marcus Licinius Crassus was becoming the richest man in Rome and a young man named Julius Caesar was beginning to make his mark on Roman society.

In detention, but not confined to a cell, Justinian was free to roam around the military camp and surrounds. Agrippa trusted the youth, and after speaking to the young Pompey, managed to secure an agreement whereupon Justinian, as a defendant, had liberty to use the resources within the camp for his defence. Technically speaking, the military camp did not suffice for the purposes of providing good defendant resources for either Justinian or Cicero. So a radius was agreed upon, encompassing Cassius's villa, Cicero's villa and

Justinian's home. Again, this plan was submitted and under Agrippa's advice, was agreed upon.

As the trial date got closer, Justinian was granted special leave of five days to prepare his defence. He wasn't sure what he should do but knew he had to visit Cassius and Scaurus. Both of these men wielded great influence throughout the Senate chamber. Justinian knew he was on good terms with both of them, although he wasn't so sure about Scaurus and his wife. He didn't wish to see Lydia again and, perhaps, Scaurus suspected something. He would visit Cassius first. However, before anything, he must visit his mother.

Attia could not remember a time when things had been so bad. Her husband gone, her son gone, her eldest daughter now a whore. Her youngest daughter, a Greckophile, totally besotted by Thucydides, Solon, Demosthenes and Homer. What had become of her family? She had lost her grip on them.

But then, she jerked. She heard the voice of her son. At last he'd come to see her. 'Justinian!' She exclaimed, rushing out of her bed chamber. 'Justinian, my darling, oh dear, look how thin you are, and what's happened to your arm?' Attia threw herself at him, almost knocking him over. She hugged him, wouldn't let go. 'Oh, my darling boy, please tell me everything is fine' and kept kissing 'Mother! Please!' Justinian yelled. She shuddered, drew back from the intensity of his voice and immediately burst into tears. He hugged her and led her into the atrium. They sat next to each other on a small bench, she sobbing quietly to herself He turned to her, 'Oh mother, please be strong for me' he implored her, 'I need you to be strong, you know I'm not capable of... He hesitated, did not want to say raping, 'killing a young girl. I was becoming quite fond of her.' Justinian put his right arm around his mother's sobbing shoulders. In a soft voice, 'Mother, please' and at the same time, his left hand gently cupped her right breast, pressing it. Attia jerked her body sideways, suddenly she was speechless, couldn't grasp the enormity of what he had just done. 'Justinian,' she cried, rearranging her night gown. 'What are you doing? You shouldn't do that' and quickly stood up. Justinian had been surprised by the firmness of his mother's breasts. 'Oh, mother, don't make a fuss, I just wanted to make you feel better,' he whispered, 'just needed to touch you as if I were your lover, let you feel how close I am to you. It was just a single moment of passionate recognition. I couldn't control it.' Attia, shocked, could only mouth something unintelligible, stormed out of the atrium, and left him alone on the bench. He didn't comprehend what she was saying but, he did hear her utter the word "girl".

Justinian left his home and quickly headed for the Scaurus 'household. He hoped the senator would be absent. The quiescent rage in his body had returned and he needed to find release, hopefully with Lydia. But Lydia wasn't present; he was ushered to Scaurus's study where the old senator was struggling with parchments. His face was a mass of creases from scowling, 'This wife of mine, all she does is spend my money. Look at these invoices, ye gods!'

'I'm sorry to hear that, sir, uh, has your wife gone out?'

'Hrrump, why's that? Do you want to see her?'

'Oh, sir, it's just to say hello, that's all,' Justinian lied.

'Well, she's in her sewing chamber. Go and say hello but whatever you say, don't tell her I'm angry about the accounts,' he demanded.

‘No, sir, just say hello and pass on my mother’s regards.’

Justinian was admitted to Lydia’s sewing chamber. Surprised, she gave him a cheery smile, ‘Hello stranger, so you’re out of detention.’ She was dressed in a simple pale green cotton shawl, over, presumably, a short tunic. As usual, Justinian found her delectable and felt his member becoming erect. Lydia detected his embarrassment and reached out to fondle his bulge. Justinian coughed, whispered, ‘Lydia, you’re such a tease, I’m getting worked-up. The senator thinks I’m just saying hello.’ She took his right hand and pressed it into her crutch. ‘There, you’re saying hello.’

There wasn’t enough time for fulfilment so the pair separated. Back with Scaurus, Justinian got his mind focused on his immediate concerns and asked the senator for his support during the trial. ‘But I cannot interfere in a court case,’ he protested.

‘Of course not, senator, but, perhaps when you are giving a speech in the chamber, you could possible add something positive about me. I’m not a killer. If it gets around that you support me, it could influence the outcome.’ Scaurus didn’t make any promises but assured Justinian he would help where appropriate. Scaurus wasn’t exactly reassuring, something had upset the old senator, and it wasn’t Lydia’s spending habits.

Cassius too, was moody. Justinian guessed it had something to do with his mother. To a degree, he could understand Cassius’s frustration. Despite the glum mood, Cassius assured Justinian that he would, where possible, try and influence his fellow senators to think positively of the youth. Cassius’s final words, however, made the most sense, ‘Leave the leading to Cicero.’

Chapter 10

The Law Courts were close to the Senate Chamber. The court was sensibly partitioned; an elevated reserve for the praetor-magistrate, the defence advocate and the prosecutor would face the selected jurors, all class-1 citizens. There were also quite a few spectators, including families present. Attia and Julia sat with Cassius while Sabina's mother sat with Agrippa. At the appropriate time, Praetor Maximus Canidius opened the proceedings by announcing the case, the Roman Republic vs Justinian Cornelia on charges of rape and malicious killing. The youth stood and faced the magistrate while the charges were called out by the court clerk.

With the proceedings underway, the prosecuting advocate, Servilius Caput, read out the charges as alleged by one Aulus Rufinius, citizen third class, a fruit and vegetable merchant of Formiae. When the charges were out, Cicero requested to examine the witness, and within a matter of moments, he demolished the witnesses' testimony, stating that the witness had broken the law by dumping the girl's body outside an abandoned warehouse. Aulus Rufinius was not a credible witness, could not be trusted with regard to his allegation, and therefore should be dismissed.

However, the prosecutor disagreed. Cicero had scored valuable points with his attempted dismissal of Aulus. But, the gentleman in question had associated with the alleged murderer, had been a companion up until the moment the young soldier had been arrested. So, if anything, Aulus should remain as a witness for the prosecution but, his allegation can be struck off.

While these arguments were taking place, Justinian from his sideways vantage position, could observe his family, those connected to the case, and the spectators who were there out of some morbid fascination to see killers being found guilty. He stared at his mother, whatever state she had been in before the trial, she had now rallied. Dressed in her finest stola, her brunette hair beautifully set with a parting in the middle, curls down to the nape of her neck in a chignon style. She looked stately and attractive, despite being in mourning for Justinian's father. The youth squirmed, next to her sat the ubiquitous Cassius. How many times had he touched her breasts, he pondered? \Next to Cassius, sat Julia, with Catalina in tow. What a pair, already rumours were rampant, what a reputation—Julia and Catalina can't contribute to my defence. If asked, he'll disown them; after all, he was the *pater familius,* head of the household.

Cicero had no more questions for Aulus Rufinius so the plaintiff was stood down. However, Cicero did want to speak to the jury concerning the plaintiff's role in this tragic tale.

Cicero opened his address by saying, 'Aulus Rufinius is a vegetable merchant and, as such, is concerned with delivery of produce and his clients. That's how he makes his living!' Cicero shouted to those present, making several in the audience jerk in their seats. '

Aulus was left with the girl's body; he was forced to get rid of the body. How could he explain her to the burial authorities? Would they believe him? The youth who was arrested at the garrison was the key to all this but he wasn't available to testify for Aulus Rufinius. So please, treat Aulus with some empathy, understand where he's coming from. Thank you.' Justinian shook his head, asked himself would Cicero expect payment from Aulus for clearing him of any wrongdoing? This trial was becoming a farce.

The next witness was the flour merchant, Gordanius, technically, another plaintiff. Cicero eyed him suspiciously before asking his first question. Justinian nodded to himself, he was definitely the man after the pony, and in charge of two thugs.

'You are a merchant too, simply known as Gordanius, right?' Cicero asked. 'That's right' Gordanius answered promptly.

'You hire men to work for you, yes?'

'Yes, as do all businessmen.'

'You've been known to hire deserting soldiers, have you not?' Cicero inquired in a more serious voice.

'I didn't know they were deserters, there's no way of knowing,' was the prompt reply.

Cicero ignored the reply and quickly asked, 'You claim that this young man over here raped and killed the young girl named Sabina?'

'I do,' was the reply.

'And what proof do you have?'

'When I got what I was after, my pony, what the girl stole, I left him and her—he was infatuated with the girl, tried to stop my men from taking the pony and slashed one of my men across the face, left a nasty wound—he's got a bad temper has that one.' Gordanius explained.

'Sir, can I ask you the question again? What proof do you have that the young man here raped and strangled the girl?'

'I didn't see him do it but he kept giving her the evil eye, I knew what his intentions were' he sardonically answered. Cicero dismissed his answer, claiming that he had no proof and that he was not a mind reader.

Justinian smiled to himself, more points to Cicero. Yes, this was all going well. By the time Cicero deals with the next two allegations, we should be finished with this trial in less than a day.

Servilius Capito rose to face the magistrate, 'Sire, I would like to call the next witness, if our brother Marcus Tullius has no objections.'

'Cicero?' The magistrate called.

'So be it, sire.'

'I'd like to call Agrippa Aurelius Cotta to the witness stand.'

Agrippa stood, then made his way to front of the courtroom. He stood in the witness partition.

'Do you promise to tell the truth, soldier?'

'I do,' was the reply.

After formal identification, Capito got down to business. 'Did Justinian of the Corneeli, aged almost seventeen, desert his troop while it was on a mission? I just want yes or no, soldier.'

'Yes,' Agrippa answered.

'What is the punishment for desertion, soldier?'

'Usually death, sire, depending on citizen status.'

'In the case of the young, Corneli, what?'

'Salt mine for life'

'So, why isn't he in a salt mine now?'

'We found he had extenuating circumstances, sire.'

'What were those circumstances, soldier?'

'He got lost.'

Suddenly there was uproar from the audience, it lasted for almost two minutes; Justinian found himself blushing from embarrassment. Well, that didn't go down too well, he considered.

Capito waited till the sniggering ceased, continued, 'How could he get lost with so many other soldiers about?'

'He went swimming and got swept downstream. He was attempting to make his way back when he was overpowered by someone, er, a stranger.'

'Do you know who this stranger is, soldier?'

'Yes, he is one of Marius's bodyguards, Theorex, a Gaul or Teuton, one of the two.'

'So, soldier, what happened to our intrepid friend next?'

The mention of Marius's name had brought a mixed reception of reactions. Cicero, shifting, jumped up and hollered, 'this information is not…'

'Oh. Cicero, be quiet!' The magistrate charged.

The great advocate slumped back into his seat, scowling.

'What next, soldier?'

'The youth remained with Marius and his bodyguard overnight.'

'Presumably, he left the next morning,' Capito offered.

'Yes, and at this stage he was cut off from the rest of his troop. They were marching south to Formiae.'

'Sire, leave the questioning of this witness for my learned colleague.'

'No questions sire.'

'In that case, let us adjourn for some lunch. Let us reconvene when the afternoon guard changes later this afternoon.' the praetor informed everyone.

Cicero swung around, 'Have you been collusive with Marius and his faction?' He demanded.

'No, I swear!' Justinian exclaimed, adding, 'Marius's Gaul bodyguard grabbed me and took me, blindfolded, to Marius's hiding place. That's the honest truth.'

'Very well, but this puts a new complexion on things. Observers think you're in the Marian faction, therefore, an enemy of Sulla,' Cicero declared.

Justinian sighed, replied, 'You've got to explain to people that meeting with Marius was by chance, not intentional. I have nothing to do with the Marian faction.'

For Justinian, things looked grim. Information from the trial went to Sulla. Learning about the Marian connection added fuel to the fire. Sitting there with a glum look on his face, staring into space, he was unexpectedly joined by his younger sister, Antonia. She squeezed onto the bench seat next to him. 'How are you, brother, things a little up and down, I hear?' He studied her young face, unblemished, thin lips, short hair, pretty in a sort of awkward way; her brown eyes probing, perhaps studying his soul and not liking what she comprehended.

`Oh, Antonia, if only I hadn't met Marius,' he uttered in a weak voice. Antonia frowned, 'I don't think Marius is your main problem,' she answered.

'Why do you say that? What is my main problem?'

'Did you inappropriately touch mother yesterday?'

Justinian bowed his head, took his eyes off Antonia. 'Yes, I touched her on the breast. I don't know why, it was done without thinking. I just wanted to feel her. Mother excites me all of a sudden, it's weird.'

'Where did you go afterwards?'

'To see Senator Scaurus for his help.'

'What about Lydia?'

Before he could answer, Praetor Canidius returned to his seat and ordered the court case to commence. He looked to the counsel and nodded to Cicero to continue. He rose, faced the jurors and said: 'I simply want to remind the jurors what this trial is about. We're here to determine whether or not this young man, Justinian, raped and maliciously killed a young girl named Sabina. Let's look at some of the facts: he has no motive for killing her, what would he gain? He felt for the young girl and wanted her to have a decent burial so he ensured she would get to the proper authorities but was stymied by the military authorities when he got back to the military camp. He carried out this task on his own volition. This is all that I have to say for the moment. Just ask my learned colleague if he wishes to introduce any more witnesses.' He nodded to the prosecutor. Capito rose from his seat and said, 'Yes, one more witness, please.' Cicero, looking a bit mystified, nodded, 'Certainly.'

Capito made his way to the front, turned and faced the jurors. 'I'd like to call the Teuton, Theorex, to the witness stand, thank you.'

Justinian, at the mention of the name, squirmed uneasily in his seat. Cicero's jaw dropped and he sat there with his mouth open. Theorex made his way to the witness stand, stood and faced the prosecutor. Capito's voice cut through the silence. Members of the audience and most of the jurors had never seen a Teuton before. He was tall, muscular and had long fair hair. His face was chiselled with a dimpled chin. 'Sire, and jurors, I want you to meet Theorex, He is a member of the Germanic tribe, the Cimbri. He was a child when Marius adopted him. His parents had been killed by Roman soldiers at the Battle of Vercellae in Gaul, fifteen years ago. He grew up to love his adopted guardian and served to protect him.'

As we all know, Marius died several days ago and Theorex brought his body to Rome to be cremated with due honours. Whatever Marius did in his last days while he was ill has largely been put aside. Theorex is heartbroken but he has something to say. He learned our language under Marius and speaks it very well.'

Theorex stood tall, facing the jurors. 'The morning the youth left us; Marius told me to follow him in case the youth returned to a body of soldiers and told them about our camp. Once the youth returned to the roadway, I was able to follow him by hiding behind trees running parallel to the roadway. It wasn't long before he met the girl with the pony coming in the opposite direction, heading towards Rome. The youth decided to escort the girl back to Rome. So, by the time, I thought it safe to return to my master.'

'However, I noticed that they pulled off the roadway and strolled through the forest until they found a spot where they could sit and have something to eat. At this stage, I was going to return to my master, but I heard the horses arriving. Horsemen tracked the couple through the growth by following their passage through bushes and impressions made on damp ground. The girl fled with the pony into denser forest. The young man here was knocked flat by a blow to the head. The girl and the pony were caught and returned to the site they were discovered. The man bringing the girl and the pony back had a large gash on his face, his clothing ruffled. The boss man let his two hired men have their own way with the girl. I couldn't see what they were doing but I heard the girl scream many times. After some time, the men left the girl, she was moaning, crying softly, and then the boss man went and looked at her. He knelt down and shook his head, then returned to his horse. They left with the pony in tow. Shortly after the men left, the young soldier got up off the ground, shook his head a number of times, found the girl and shouted obscenities to the sky—his gods, I guess. He then knelt down and started hitting the girl with his fists until he had little energy left.

At this juncture, the audience and jurors groaned as one. Justinian slumped on the bench. Cicero got up and straightened the youth up, admonished him for revealing his feelings, told him to sit up. Capito rose out of his seat, 'Theorex, why did you not stop the youth when he started hitting the girl?'

'Sir, I am honour-bound to keep my master safe. If Romans want to kill each other, let them. There may have been other soldiers in that forest, only the day before, a squad of them was marching south. I couldn't risk it.'

'Do you think the young soldier ended the girl's life?' Capito asked. 'Yes,' was the reply, adding, 'he hit her many times and kept shouting her name.'

'Thank you, Theorex. Does my colleague want to question this witness?' Cicero shook his head, 'No, but I would like to question the defendant, Justinian Cornelaii.'

Justinian took a deep breath and got up from the bench, walked to the front and faced the audience. Justinian now noticed how much the audience had grown. The word had gotten out; this trial was worth looking at.

'So, you went for a paddle in the stream, but were caught-up by the current and carried downstream, then you were, what, hit on the head, rendered useless in a headlock, or held under water, what?' Cicero asked. 'He held my arm up my back, his other arm was around my neck, choking me,' Justinian answered.

'And he blindfolded you, took you to Marius and you remained there overnight, correct.'

'Yes sir.'

And, the questions continued for most of the afternoon. When it got to Justinian receiving the blow to the head, aspects of the defence's case changed.

'You remember being hit and blacking out, but you don't remember getting up after the horsemen left. You don't remember kneeling over the girl and hitting her?' Cicero demanded.

'No, I don't remember doing that, and if I did, I would have bruised hands and fingers, wouldn't I?'

'That is a good point, Justinian,' Cicero declared, a wry smile finding its way on his face.

'Was there any sexual activity between you and the girl? Did you attempt to touch her at all?'

Justinian frowned, clearly confused, he did touch her. I tried to stop some of the bleeding. She was bleeding down below, I tried to use some of her garments to block the bleeding, and suddenly the bleeding stopped. I believe this was when she actually died. I couldn't find any pulses.'

'Have you any medical training?' Cicero asked.

'Since I've been involved in training in the army, I have had a number of lessons on assisting the wounded, such as stemming blood flow and checking pulses to determine if a person is alive or not.'

'Of course, emergency procedures,' Cicero replied, nodding.

'Yes sir.'

Cicero went quiet for a few moments, stared at Justinian, then looked at the prosecutor, 'Do you wish to question the youth?'

'Only two questions,' he answered.

Cicero nodded. Capito made his way towards Justinian.

'Question one; do you visit Lydia Scaurus often?'

Justinian blushed, lost for words, mumbled, 'Uh, oh, not, I mean, er, not often.'

'Could you explain what you mean by not often.' Capito persisted.

'Only three or four times in the last two seasons. I mainly wanted to see Senator Scaurus.'

'On one occasion you spent quite a bit of time alone with Lydia, is this correct?'

Cicero rose from his seat, 'Objection, sire! What does this have to do with case?'

'Carry on, Capito,' the praetor ruled.

'Your answer to the last question, soldier,' Capito reminded the youth. 'We made love' Justinian declared.

There was an audible reaction among the audience. Capito waited till the chatter stopped. 'Question two; did you try to touch your mother yesterday?'

'Yes' Again, another rise in chatter from the shocked audience.

'No more questions sire.' Capito returned to his seat.

Cicero rose, 'No questions sire.'

The praetor looked to the jurors, 'Gentlemen, I would like you to cast your votes now. There are two serious matters that need voting on. One, is the defendant guilty of rape of the young girl called Sabina and, two, is the defendant guilty on the charge of malicious killing of the young girl called Sabina. Gentlemen, your votes.

It took some time to get the tokens collected and recorded by the court clerk. He handed the praetor a parchment. The praetor studied it, then announced, 'On the charge of rape, Absolvo! On the charge of malicious killing, Absolvo!'

Justinian almost fell off the bench, but managed to get back up. He thanked Jupiter for the outcomes. Then turned to Cicero, thanked him and turned towards his mother and sisters. Julia and Antonia hugged him, congratulated him and welcomed him back to the fold. His mother remained cool but did express her happiness at his acquittal.

Chapter 11

The ordeal wasn't over. Justinian was informed he would have to come back to court as a witness for the prosecution in the trial of the two hired men for raping Sabina. He was keen to say his piece, but he'd have to wait for another week before this could happen. After a congratulatory reunion with Agrippa, the two headed back to the military camp to resume soldiering. Justinian was informed he was no longer confined to quarters but questions needed answers, concerning his encounter with Marius and the slave Theorex.

When his first release from duties arrived, he headed home. He needed to rectify the damage done to the relationship with his mother. He thought long and hard about how he would do this but once he arrived home, he received a shock. His mother actually apologised to him. Looking her best, wearing a colourful pallas, she hugged him and said sorry. They would talk later, she said. For the moment then, Justinian circulated among the family His sisters were happy for him, there was no sign of Catalina, so he was happy for them. Julia was her usual flouncy self; she was everywhere. Antonia, however, appeared removed, her head in another parchment probably. 'What are you reading these days?' he asked her, giving the impression he was genuinely interested.

‘Oh, something light, for a change. I’m reading Democritus and his study of atomism, have you heard of him?’ she offered. He shook his head, frowned, ‘Sounds interesting, our Greek friends again. Are you still angry with me?’ He asked, genuinely wanting to repair any damage to relationships.

She adopted her intense scrutiny look, ‘Justinian, I was never angry with you, I simply could not understand your behaviour. I know now that, as a male, you are experiencing some profound changes in your body. These changes are of a sexual nature, and, they will influence you to do some silly things.’

‘Such as having a desire to touch mother on the breast,’ he offered. Antonia blushed, nodded, ‘Yes. That could be part of it. But I’m thinking more along the lines of visiting Lydia Scaurus for sex. She’s old enough to be your grandmother!’

‘Yes, it’s odd. I do have a desire for older women. I cannot explain it except to add that older women are more discrete about their relationships and are not given to boasting like young girls.’

‘Not all young women behave like that, I certainly wouldn’t,’ she replied. It suddenly struck Justinian that he’d never viewed his younger sister with a critical eye. He studied her now; tallish, short hair, a pretty elliptical face with piercing big brown eyes. Her body was somewhat gangling, with the buds of her breasts making an impression through her shawl. Justinian looked away; the nagging rage was returning again, he felt he was blushing. Antonia noticed his discomfort and understood what was taking place in his body. Justinian was being driven by something out of his control, Antonia knew she needed to be strong, held herself in front of him and stared at him.

Chapter 12

The episode lasted the length of eight breaths, wry short. Justinian shied away from embarrassment. Antonia watched as he displayed his awkwardness. 'Let me go, I'll keep out of everybody's way.' Justinian meekly pleaded.

'Why should you, brother, we love you.' Antonia almost shouted, as she followed his movements. He made his way to the atrium and sat on the bench overlooking the goldfish pond. Antonia sat next to him. He could smell her rosewater scent; it had a soothing effect on him. 'I love you, sister, and thank you for helping me through this ordeal.' She took his right hand and pressed it against her left breast. He felt her bud, ran his finger around its petite swell and felt his member becoming stiff. 'Ye gods,' he exclaimed in a whisper. Antonio lowered her head onto his shoulder and relaxed her body, his gentle massaging of her breast began lulling her sense of reality. 'What have the atomists to say about this?' He asked, being flippant. 'Nothing, absolutely nothing.' she offered, purring like a contented kitten.

Catalina had the right building. The tenement was conspicuous by its ruined facade. The whitewash was peeling all over the front. The building needed to be demolished, but it was occupied by at least thirty families. The owner of the tenement, Marcus Licinius Crassus, was, nowadays, one of the richest men in Rome. Crassus wanted the occupiers of the building out so he could demolish and rebuild. Those in residence had nowhere to go, but that didn't matter to Crassus, so he hired Catalina, who had contacts within the more nefarious Subura street gangs, to force these families out. So Catalina waited for his hired gang to arrive.

The first to arrive was a swarthy, heavy set man who introduced to Catalina as Gordianus. Catalina studied the man's face and announced, 'Where have I met you before?'

Gordianus related how he'd been in court, had made an allegation against the young cadet officer but his allegation had been dismissed. Now the authorities had his hired men in detention for the rape and the only witness being the cadet officer. Would the senator help in shutting up the cadet officer? There was a good possibility the senator could help, how much was Gordianus offering? Before any negotiations took place, a mob of thugs walked around the corner of the tenement building. Carrying wooden rods and the odd short sword, the group presented a formidable obstacle if you wanted to pass by it. 'Who are these?' Gordianus asked. 'Don't worry, they belong to me. They've a job to do in this tenement building.'

Catalina faced the men, gestured them to shut up and pay attention. 'You know what you have to do. Scare the occupants out of the building. What I don't want to see is women and children hurt. Do your job and do it properly. All occupants out! I even want the dogs and rats out! Pay you when the job's finished.' He dismissed the men and turned his attention back to the flour merchant. 'Look stop wasting time, if you want the youth's family shaken up, the 'cost will be ten denarii.' Catalina informed him.

'I only want them roughed up so they'll drop the case. I don't want you to support them in exile for ten years.'

'Be careful, my good man. Or we might have to rough you up.' Catalina spat back. Gordianus, clearly impressed with this man's powerful reach, decided to keep quiet.

Meanwhile, the noise and chaos in the tenement began producing results. Men, women and children, scrambling and screaming, were tossing themselves out of the front doors onto street. Catalina decided it was time to move to another location, he couldn't get himself implicated in this melee. The pair strolled peacefully across the roadway while panicked people smacked into each other, looking for somewhere to hide. 'Typical,' said Catalina, 'most of these people are squatters and layabouts. No wonder Crassus wants the place emptied,' he added. The gang of thugs had done a good job; they started boarding up the doorways and vents. Catalina, well pleased, put his arm around Gordianus's shoulder so they could discuss a plan for Justinian Cornelius's family.

Chapter 13

Back at the Field of Mars, the occupants of one tent decided to eat their evening meal together. It was really a gesture to welcome back the youth into the military fold once more. The three other occupants had managed to get hold of venison so it was cooked and served with gravy, chickpeas and potatoes. The four cadet officers chewed their way through the meal and left talking until later. Afterwards, with watered wine, they chatted about the army, families and politics. Justinian steered the conversation to women. 'Have you chaps got women to marry?' The laughter answering this question told him what the general attitude about women was. `Seriously, it's important that I know what your attitudes are for women in your lives,' he said, over the laughter. Lucius Julius, however, detected his friend is desirous of knowing about our attitudes towards the fairer sex.' he declared with a raised voice. The sniggering died; three pairs of eyes stared, a serious note to Justinian's inquiry. 'Wait, fellows, I believe our young friend is having problems with sex.' Suddenly he went quiet, blushed and responded with a shrug.

All of the cadets sat on their bunks, their thoughts dwelling on their own attitudes towards women. 'Honestly, I worship the ground that women tread on,' said Fulvius

Antonius, I mean, I just go weak at the knees if a woman came up to me and wanted to talk.'

'I believe you have to put a woman in her place, if you are going to marry her,' said Marcus Pius in a deep voice. Two heads nodded, 'let's face it, none of us is ready to marry, we're too young. I like getting women into bed,' ventured Pedianus Fuscus, adopting a lofty air.

This was Justinius's cue, 'so, you are all for sex, Pedianus?'

'Well, I haven't met a girl, who didn't want it,' Pedianus replied.

'In my family, I'm surrounded by women,' Justinian offered.

'But they're not there for sex, not family,' Fulvius interjected.

'I made love to my younger sister last night,' Justinian confessed.

The group went quiet, all eyes, once more, on the youth. 'Sex is usually for outside the family. Don't think I could do that to my sister.' said Lucius Julius. Justinian nodded, 'my sister wanted it, we both wanted it, it just happened. It was good.'

'I'm for turning in, what about you fellows?' Pedianus said, fighting back a yawn.

'The gods forbid that sort of thing, you know,' Marcus Pius informed them. 'In fact, it's punishable by death in the religious world.'

'Justinian, you need to have words with the Pontiff Maximus,' Lucius said, getting up to go to his bunk. 'Good night, fellows, I'm for sleep,' he announced.

After midnight, the military camp becomes quiet except for the odd order being shouted by a guard somewhere, or the braying of mules, natter of horses. A soldier was running, making his way to Justinian's tent. Once there, he called for the youth. Justinian, rubbing his eyes, awoke, 'Sir, that you? I'm awake, what's the problem?' He called, knowing Agrippa was waiting outside. An officer can only enter a cadet's tent during daylight hours. Justinian rushed outside the tent, 'What's the problem, sir?' he yelled. Agrippa grabbed him by the arm. 'We've just heard that your house is on fire. You'd better be off and see if you can render your family any help.' Agrippa explained. Justinian scowled, then took off.

By the time Justinian reached his street, his home-villa was a pile of smouldering rubble. Men were still running back and forth with wooden buckets filled with water but the embers were relentless, billowing smoke still issued from the rear rooms. 'Does anyone know where my family is?' He shouted. 'With Cassius,' was the quick reply. Justinian bowed his head, thanked Jupiter.

There was nothing he could have done. There was nothing to save. Totally gutted, even the goldfish had boiled to death. Justinian started making his way to Cassius's residence, not far from the forum.

Banging on the huge wooden door brought Alexander, Cassius's only slave; he quickly ushered in the youth. Standing together in the main lounging room were mother, and the two sisters, appearing unhurt but covered from head to foot in soot while Munius desperately tried to tidy-up the women by constantly rubbing the soot away, though the women were oblivious to his efforts. For a moment, Justinian felt like laughing, but for the seriousness of the evening's events, he resisted the urge. 'Mother, what happened? Was it an accident, was anyone hurt?' He shouted without taking a breath. Cassius rushed into the room to find out what the commotion was about. 'Ah. Justinian, your mother and sisters are fine, and so are the slaves,' he bellowed. Justinian went straight to his mother and hugged her, she laid her head on his shoulder, exhausted; he caressed her cheek, 'We'll get back on top, mother. I promise.' She spoke, 'Where are we going to stay? Please tell me, where are we going to stay? You are the pater familias in our family. You must find us a place where we can live in safety!' she exclaimed, her head still on his shoulder. She whispered, 'Dignitas, dignitas, dignitas…'

Chapter 14

'Someone was seen sneaking around the villa last night before the fire started. So, yes, I'd say someone is after you and your family. Who do you know that hates you or your family?' Agrippa asked. 'It's got to be connected to the testimony I'm going to give against the flour merchant and his two hired bullies, they want me to back off.' Justinian quickly realised.

'Yes, that makes sense. You've got to bring those evil bastards to justice. By the way, where is your family staying?'

'With Cassius, his home is more like a palace; he even declined any rent,' Justinian explained.

Agrippa nodded, 'That's good, now, back to Gordanius and his lackeys. Gordanius is a free man, while his lackeys are being held in detention until trial. I know someone who may be able to help us. And, I know you know him. Senator Catalina.'

'Ah him, the oaf! Yes, if there's one man in this city who knows anything. It's the oaf! He and my sister were close for a period, but she dropped him—found him to be too furtive, always up to something.'

'Yes, I have the same opinion of him too, after we had that chat the evening before we left for Capua.'

'Let's pay him a visit. Sir, we need to have a talk about his involvement in these gangs,' Justinian replied.

Catalina's office was located near the Temple of Diana. As Agrippa and Justinian arrived, they found at least twenty clients waiting to see the senator. Disappointed, Agrippa sought out the senator's secretary. Once found, Antiochus, a Greek slave, arranged a meeting for the pair after the current client finished his business with the senator. After greeting the pair, Agrippa didn't waste any time. 'We could have you up on three charges before you even opened your mouth,' Agrippa shouted.

Catalina didn't show any concern over the officer's angry outburst. 'Please lower your voice, officer, or you will alarm my clients. You wouldn't want me to go to Sulla with a complaint, would you?' the senator calmly replied.

'Sir, I believe you have been personally complicit in several crimes against citizens of Rome,' Agrippa declared.

'Evidence, officer, have you any?' Cataline asked.

'I'll get evidence. I know that you've been profiting through proscription confiscations. I'm sure Sulla would not welcome that news,' Agrippa spat back.

Catalina's face suddenly took on a frowning mask of concern, 'Rubbish, the authorities can check my ledgers, there's nothing untoward there. And, Sulla knows I'm an agent for his collections. I personally work under the direction of Marcus Licinius Crassus. Do you hear me, soldier? What bloody hope have you got taking me in front of the criminal courts?' he demanded, adding, 'I am one of Sulla's favourites!'

Agrippa wasn't put off by Catalina's boasting, 'Sir, get rid of your clients, I'm taking you to the garrison for questioning, now.'

Agrippa called for two guards; they took the senator by the arms. He yelled, 'Tiro, tell the clients to come back tomorrow. Get Cornelius Lentulus, tell him I'll be at the military garrison, The Field of Mars.'

Tiro, shocked at his master's arrest, bowed dutifully to Cataline, nodded at the instructions. 'Yes, master, I'll get Lentulus straight away.'

Once outside, Catalina ceased his protesting and proudly held his head in the air as four soldiers marched him towards The Field of Mars. Tiro, meanwhile, raced off in the opposite direction to find Lentulus. Catalina's clients stood in a group, whispering among themselves, disturbed over their patron's arrest.

On arrival at the garrison, Catalina was promptly thrown into a dungeon. Owing to his status, he was left unchained, but didn't stop protesting, and demanding to see Sulla. Concern now showed on Agrippa's face. Shortly, he'd have to face Lentulus, Catalina's lawyer. Agrippa had no warrant and, at this stage, the senator in the dungeon was here for questioning. Agrippa stood in front of the dungeon door, 'Will you ever close that mouth of yours? If you do so, I'll inform you why you were brought here.' Clearly the prefect of the garrison was angry. 'You're a fool, Catalina! Did you arrange a deal with Gordianus? Arrange to help him to get the youth, Justinian, to withdraw his testimony, know anything about this?'

Catalina went quiet.

Agrippa now laid out the three charges against Cataline.

'Charge number one: did escort a minor to a banned religious festival celebrating a debauched Bacchus. Charge number two: did knowingly have sexual relations with a minor, knowing she was under age. Charge number three: you did knowingly profiteer from Sulla's proscription procedures by claiming possession of an assortment of valuable early Greek vases and statuettes. Here we have two moral' charges and one fraud charge; witnesses for every event.' Agrippa went quiet, allowed Catalina time to think 'Well, Catalina, what do you plead? Charge one, the banned festival.'

'Guilty.' Cataline whispered.

'Charge two, sex with a minor.'

'Guilty.'

'Charge three, fraud through workplace.'

'Not guilty.'

Agrippa felt himself wanting to grin, but he desisted. Just as well. Because Lentulus had just this instant walked into the garrison.

Chapter 15

Because Agrippa had no authority to arrest Catalina, the senator was released from custody. Lentulus demanded a written apology. However, by this stage, Catalina had agreed to cooperate with Agrippa and answer some important questions about the arson attack on Justinian's home. As usual, Lentulus, as Catalina's defence lawyer, was totally in the dark concerning the senator's nefarious dealings. Why had Catalina now emboldened himself, despite the criminal and fraud charges levelled against him? For two important reasons: Marcus Lucinius Crassus and Lucius Cornelius Sulla, his friends.

Agrippa sat down at his heavy wooden desk and put his mind to work, attempting to steer his way to a sensible outcome. As an army officer, he had powerful friends. But now he asked himself, who could he really count on? He could count on Cassius, he couldn't count on Lucullus for he was Sulla's man, he couldn't count on Crassus for he was his own man. He couldn't count on Carbo or Cinna because they were Marian's at heart. Agrippa suddenly found very, little room to manoeuvre in. But today, he had learned, from Catalina that Gordianus had sought help from the senator and had been directed to some Subura tavern where he met a seedy individual known as “the knife”. This individual would burn down Justinian’s household for a fee. Agrippa was just beginning to get his mind around these facts when an officer legate entered Agrippa’s office space. ‘Afternoon, prefect, apologies for interrupting but some urgent news has come through from Greece.’

‘What urgent news?’ Agrippa asked.

‘Lucius Murena is getting a few legions together. We’re on the warpath again against Mithridates, our old friend. Your legion will be shipping out tonight.’

Chapter 16

The Field of Mars was teeming with activity: soldiers, horses, mules, and ballista. Nothing stands still in time of war; the sweat and tears of hundreds of days of activities comes together for the march. The legions would march to Brundisi, board ships for Greece. Under the command of Sulla's appointed legate, Lucius Morena, the Romans would march across Cappadocia and attack Mithridates in the, town of Comana.

Agrippa spent the rest of the afternoon preparing for battle. Only his IVth legion was selected, which included Justinian, who had just cast off his mantle of cadet, and now was recognised as an acting cadet officer. Justinian would take his place in the cohort's command structure to make sure soldiers were properly prepped; their weapons cleaned and ready for use, soldiers knew their role in the cohort tactics. As an adjunct, Justinian was also responsible for his cohort's mules, making sure they were fed, shod, and in good health for the long marches.

Justinian's feelings about the assignment were mixed. He would have to postpone his court appearances until he returned. The two thugs in detention would get their freedom back and escape justice. His mother and two sisters were living in someone's house. They had very little clothing or personal effects. 'Jupiter!' He cussed, 'things are looking bad.'

Soldiers rallied to their marching positions. It took some time for the 5,000 plus men to line up and dress down, six abreast, creating a snake-like line almost two times lengthier than the whole camp itself. Marching commenced just before sunset and it would take almost ten days to reach Brundisium. Marching in heavy leather sandals with hobnails on the soles, it wasn't long before blisters started to appear, but there was no stopping the IVth legion under Pompey. The youth, Justinian, as a sworn officer, now wore the full garb: crested helmet, greaves for his shins, armour plates for shoulders and chest, red cloak and red tunic underneath. Justinian felt proud wearing the colours of his legion. The IVth legion had a long and honourable history. Dating back some hundred years, the legion underwent many structural changes during the generalship of Marius. The legion's first major battle honours were won during the Germanic invasions of thirty years ago. The Battle of Aquae Sextia and The Battle of Vercellae were two huge victories for Giaus Marius and his Roman legions. Marius went on to become consul of Rome six times. His seventh consulship was considered unconstitutional. But Marius spoke highly of the IVth.

Brundisium is absolute chaos. After the ten-day march, most soldiers are worn ragged with an assortment of skin wounds from boils to sweat rashes. Now they board ships and spend eight days at sea, battling sea sickness. The mules are on board, the soldiers are on board, and the stores are on board. Justinian is on board and learns that officer accommodation is fully taken. He settles with other soldiers on the deck, hoping the night breeze will improve things. It doesn't, as Optio, his rank is not important but the men make room for him. Early in the morning, he stirred, vomited, rolled over and went back to sleep. When he awoke, Justinian felt terrible; the motion of the boat: up, down, crash; another wave crashes over the bows. 'Oh, Jupiter,' he moans, and simply hopes that nobody is looking for him. But Agrippa is looking for him with important news.

Chapter 17

Five days of torture, his stomach feels like a dried out, wrung leather drinking bladder. All he can do is drink water and swallow small bits of crust. However, today is a reprieve; early this morning, land mass is sighted, Greece grows bigger by the day. Justinian decides he'd better make his presence felt, so wrestles with himself to rally what's left of his strength to locate Agrippa. Finally, among five hundred soldiers, many still seasick, the two meet.

`Oh dear, ooh, dear Jupiter, spare me this torture. I'm so sorry, sir, I'm not much of a sailor, eh,'

Agrippa nodded, 'Never mind, I've got some news you might respond to.'

'What news?'

Agrippa leaned in closer, 'Our two friends, responsible for raping the girl, they've been pressed into service, they're on board this vessel,' he whispered.

'Ye gods, are you sure? It's not normal practice for the army to press detainees into service, is it?'

'The legion is short of men; therefore we recruit ex-soldiers where ever we can find them. We needed to fill the ranks, so they're auxiliaries, foot-sloggers.'

Suddenly, Justinian's seasickness decreased, 'Indeed, this is very interesting news, sir, what exactly is Lucius Murena up to?'

'Sulla left Commander Murena here to make sure Mithridates kept to his end of the bargain. Mithridates has commenced recruiting, and is also building a fleet of ships, ready for an invasion. He's not happy with just Pomtus, he's after Asia Minor and this time he's got rebellious Greeks to help him. So, Murena has to prevent this from escalating into all-out war. Murena has only two legions, his and ours. The VIIIth and the IVth, that's all we've got' Agrippa paused, then added, 'But do you know what the real problem is?'

Justinian shook his head.

'This task force, our legion included, does not have the permission of the Senate for a strike against Mithridates. So we're out here illegally,'

'Holy Jupiter, more troubles!' Justinian exclaimed.

Piraeus, the port, was a seething mass of humanity and animals. Junior officers were busy counting their cohorts. A number of soldiers had died during the sea voyage. This was attributed to weak constitutions and serious sea-sickness. Mules died too, due to cramped conditions, damp and lack of regular feeding. Despite this, the legions disembarked, marched across Cappodecia with the intention of sacking the township of Cobana.

Athens is a spectacular city for its layout and design. The old architecture says a lot about the intellect that used to occupy this city, Justinian thought, but there's still widespread damage from the Spartan invasion of many years ago. How he wished his sister, Antonia, was here; she'd be able to explain how the Spartans gained entry into the city, got to the citadel while the Athenians were dropping like flies from disease and starvation. But Athens was just a stepping stone in the mind of the Roman commander, Murena. From here, it was another sea trip to Ephesus, then overland to Cabana.

Chapter 18

Justinian was shocked at the extent of poverty in these Middle Eastern lands. And yet, the kings or potentates were drowning in riches. The rulers paid for their armies, built fleets, devastated towns and villages, murdered thousands. Interbreeding was the norm in these countries. Royal blood was sacrosanct and must be protected at all costs.

Agrippa is of the opinion that the whole scenario of this war with Mithridates is wrong. 'We have no mandate to attack these people. There has been no breaking of peace terms. Murena knows that Mithridates is arming his forces and building a fleet to deal with Colchis rebellion forces and the tribes around Cimmarian Bosphorus. Murena is seizing on an opportunity to trounce Mithridates and claim more territory for Rome. Murena also knows there is a great deal of loot to be had from the many villages in Asia Minor' Agrippa explained, then added, 'As soldiers, it's our duty to obey orders. But when these orders come from an incompetent commander, what do we do? We follow orders regardless, and try our best to make the experience a positive one.' Agrippa shook his head, confounded over the whole operation.

Murena had his soldiers sack each village as they made their way to Cabana. The commander took what he fancied:

gold pieces, carvings, statuettes, rugs, silk, anything of value. It was during these activities that Justinian caught sight of the two ex-gladiators, soldiers now auxiliaries, enjoying their new occupation of bullying villagers to hand over their valuables. The youth was so inflamed with anger, he was just about to go over and give the pair a reprimand when he was pulled back by Agrippa. 'Wait, you cannot say anything to the pair, they have been authorised to behave like this to the villagers.' he cautioned Justinian.

Agrippa learned that envoys from the Senate in Rome arrived and their task was to advise Commander Murena to uphold the truce with Mithridates. The sacking and looting of villages in Poritus was considered illegal, and that Murena should return to Rome immediately. Murena ignored the official Senate decree to back off and attacked Corbana. Mithridates saw this as Roman aggression, breaking the truce. He retaliated. Murena was defeated, and fled to Phrigia with the remains of his two legions. Justinian and Agrippa, as part of the bedraggled IVth legion arrived safely, following Murena.

Justinian, after his first taste of battle, was so unnerved; he couldn't think straight He fought bravely, leading his cohort from the front. He dispensed with his javelin very early in the attack, failing to hit anything. With sword and shield, he pushed forward and applied his training to the point where he managed to severely wound three of his opposite number. Because he showed valour in his charging, rallying his own contingent of soldiers, he was mentioned in dispatches. Agrippa too, led from the front. Putting his reservations aside, he attacked with ruthless dexterity, killing and maiming many. However, after a protracted conflict, the Romans knew they were losing the battle. Mithridates' numbers were too great; the Romans were slowly falling back and within the passage of the morning, the battle was over and the Romans, defeated.

Murena, despite the rout, refused to admit defeat. He believed that Mithridates had received a bloody nose and would think twice about warring with Romans. Agrippa saw no logic in Murena's interpretation of the battle. He, similar to the rest of the body of Romans, felt the sting of Murena's misplaced view of the battle. 'How can this defeat be considered a victory,' he hollered to no one in particular. He was disgusted, but praised the efforts of his own cohorts. It was a shameful display of Roman incompetence, costing many lives, gaining nothing. The only one to walk away with any bounty was the commander.

The Roman dead were left there to be picked to bits by the buzzards and vultures. A shameful humiliation, Agrippa declared to his fellow officers. 'Make sure the Senate knows what took place here,' he ordered, 'I'll not be a willing party to this defeat.' But Agrippa's denunciation didn't last long, he was ordered by a senior officer to refrain from criticising until they got back to Rome. Agrippa complied, but under severe strain.

Eight days after the battle, what was left of the legions joined their ships for a voyage back to Ephesus. Counting of the dead and missing was carried out under the strenuous conditions of boarding the vessels and having to store ship with food items and new livestock for the voyage back to Rome. The sailing back to Rome took five weeks and was uneventful, seas were calm, the weather balmy, men relaxed on the decks, sang, talked about bawdy encounters, played checkers, a few got their hands on wine but couldn't fool their seniors. Officers were reluctant to press petty charges. Morale was still pretty low from their first blooding and subsequent retreat.

Whenever possible, Agrippa and Justinian talked and kept their attention focused on their two auxiliary friends, who, for the length of the voyage, largely kept to themselves. Justinian, having the most opportunities to witness their activities, began to sense something strange about their behaviour. The pair was beginning to circulate around all the accommodation areas of the ship. They were talking to small groups of soldiers. Justinian decided to investigate. He borrowed some soldier's garb and hung around with some auxiliaries near the forecastle. The pair soon made their appearance and began denouncing the commander's action. Soon, they got onto the fact that a lot of the commander's loot was stowed aboard this very ship. Why don't they mutiny and steal the ship? Join some real pirates and hide away somewhere in the Greek islands with the intention of robbing the Egyptian fleet, they'd make a fortune. A lot of the listeners were becoming comfortable with this treasonous talk.

Rather than sleeping that night, Justinian decided to think about what the traitors might be doing. In his foot-soldier garb, he wandered around the deck listening for the mutinous pair. They were in the aft mess, persuading a small group of soldiers to jump the skipper of this boat and make a course for the nearest Greek island. Justinian heard the soldiers yelling for action, so he rushed down, aft, and warned the officer of the watch that there was an armed rebellion aboard his ship. He, in turn, alerted the skipper. At this juncture, the boat began changing its course to the south-east. A mob of about twelve soldiers, armed with their short swords, swarmed around the hapless helmsman and made sure the vessel stayed on its south-easterly course. Justinian sneaked off to the quarterdeck, but stopped suddenly; he just managed to glimpse Agrippa and three other officers being held at sword point. And, for the second time in his life, Justinian blacked out as a metal, leather cosh found its mark on the back of his head.

Waking up was a painful procedure as Justinian tried to focus on what was before him. Agrippa was next to him and scattered around were another six senior ranks. This represented the total compliment of officers on the vessel. The mutineers had been successful in securing the boat, and with a new heading, on their way back to the nearest Greek island. Justinian's headache was affecting his ability to work out what was going on. Agrippa took his wrist and squeezed it to reassure him he would be safe. They are all in a tiny cabin, probably the mate's quarters. The desk has been pushed aside and several officers were tied up, their arms behind their backs. Two foot soldiers were guarding the door. They were armed with short swords.

As Justinian finally came around, Agrippa explained what was happening. 'We're being taken to an island and we're going to be used for ransom money. In other words, they'll demand a hundred denarii for the likes of me. That means my parents will have to fork out 100 denarii to have me returned.'

'You will have fifty denarii on your head.'

'My mother won't have fifty denarii.' Justinian replied.

Chapter 19

Agrippa looked up at the men guarding the door. 'Do you men realise what consequences will result of all this stupidity?' The guards told him to shut up. But the officer just continued, 'No I didn't think you did. This could result in crucifixion or decimation; take your pick, men.' The guards looked at each other, swallowed hard, but said nothing. 'Think about it men, hanging on a cross while your limbs snap one at a time, or being beaten to death by your fellow soldiers.'

'Shut up you! You're just full of bullshit!' the guard screamed.

'We'll soon see who is full of bullshit.' Agrippa was about to get to his feet, but Justinian restrained him.

'Sir, just drop it. There's two swords against your bare hands.'

'These fools will never get away with it,' Agrippa spat.

Despite what Agrippa believed, the boat made it to an island east of Chios. Small, rocky, and nobody on board knowing the name, the island had numerous bays where vessels could shelter from storms at sea. The island seemed uninhabited; vegetation and fresh water were in abundance. Mutineers gathered on shore, while the captives remained on board and details about their next of kin recorded. There were about forty captives, under the tight control of twenty-five mutineers. A selected group of mutineers started sifting through the loot belonging to Commander Murena.

Murena's loot didn't amount to much. The mutineers were very disappointed, so they got to work to bring in some ransom money. A contingent of sailors was selected to sail the ship to Athens. There, they would provide the Roman authorities with the names of valuable senatorial captives and the ransoms demanded for their freedom. All up, the ransoms would be a tidy sum. There was plenty of fresh water on the island and the mutineers soon discovered feral livestock eating from the bushes. A large hog was killed for the first night's meal. One aspect of the mutiny, thus far, had been overlooked: there was no appointed leader. Most of the mutineers were content to do their own thing, carefully watching each other. Since arriving on the island, Agrippa has counted twenty-four mutineers and thirty-eight captives. Of this figure, only fourteen captives had their hands tied behind their backs. This figure obviously represents high risk potential. Agrippa and Justinian, fortunately, were considered low risk. So, the pair sat around and put their minds to work.

Later that night, the pair had a plan, but it was a matter of waiting for the right moment. The new day dawned with Agrippa and Justinian strolling around the island in deep discussion. They settled on a plan and returned to try and get some breakfast. Last night's hog provided some scrapings of meat, so the pair was content to sit and listen to the murmurings of the mutineers. The next morning would see a contingent set sail for Athens to hand over the ransom notices to the Roman governor.

Justinian, by nature, wasn't a sneaky person. But today, he decided to be different, and while he was on his morning stroll, he suddenly darted sideways when he was adjacent to the boat. Nobody saw him do this; therefore, nobody saw him go down a ladder to the lower deck and see the blackness of the bilge area swallow him up. Justinian was on board, drank some water from a bladder. Then curled up and remained quiet.

A short time later, a group of six mutineers descended on the boat and readied the vessel for sea. Estimates were four days at the most to reach Athens. By mid-morning, the vessel was about eight leagues out and going about a snail's pace through the calm ocean towards the west-south-west. Justinian spent time in quiet conversation with Jupiter, his higher power. By the end of that first day, the youth dug into his tunic and brought out his first meal of crispy hog skin, he wolfed it down, curled up and went to sleep.

The following morning, the men on board, knew that all the estimates were wrong. Sight of the Greek mainland was straight ahead. Another day or so would see Athens. The mutineers smiled to themselves, being a pirate was easier than they thought. They sailed into Piraeus harbour, marvelling at the Parthenon, gloating at them from its hilltop. A scurry of activity by the mutineers saw the vessel tied alongside a small pier. Justinian decided to move to a more secluded spot. As the men were all occupied on deck, the youth moved slowly through the narrow corridors below the top deck. He found a closet and moved in. The inside was cluttered with sail cloth, bits of wood, woodworking tools and amphorae of varnish and tar. Justinian squeezed himself into folded sailcloth, and made sure it covered the length of his body. He was inside a locker of sorts, and he was well pleased with his efforts.

Next morning, the crew were up and about. Some had already set off for the Roman governor's office. A skeleton crew were left on board; they mainly lazed around waiting for their fellow mutineers to return. Justinian, hardly hearing any movement aboard the vessel, knew it was time to move. Extracting himself from the sailcloth, he eased open the door and looked for any sign that someone was nearby. All clear, he moved out of the closet and headed for the nearest ladder. Quietly negotiating one step at a time, he made it to the top. He now had a view straight to the forecastle. Two mutineers stood chatting with their backs to him. The gangplank to the wharf was directly behind the two. Justinian didn't stop to think about it, he charged to the right and quickly hopped over the side rail, landing with a splash in the cool harbour water. The pair turned, raced to the guardrail and stared at the youth swimming away from the ship. They were helpless to do anything, they couldn't swim. With a shrug of the shoulders, they turned and resumed their conversation. They wouldn't say anything to the others.

The shock of the cold water soon wore off. Justinian had had swimming lessons so he soon got his body into a freestyle motion and glided through the water until, still holding his breath, he stopped and then let his feet do the work to keep him stable so he could see what was happening around him. Head above water, he was surprised nobody was in the water; he was alone among many ships. Breast-stroking, he slowly made his way to the wharf and quickly found a pole and rafters he could climb. Once on the wharf, he sat down and recovered his energy. Nobody took any notice of him. He was soaked to the skin and started to think about getting dry. It was a beautiful morning, sun shining, it wouldn't take long, he had to get away from these buildings and ships. He walked down the side of a warehouse, out into an open field. Some livestock were grazing, corralled in a roped off area. He wouldn't look conspicuous near the livestock. He stripped to his tunic and placed his other garments over the ropes. Sitting down, he grabbed a long blade of grass and chewed on it.

Chapter 20

The drying process was taking too long. Justinian put his military tunic back on, his cold weather breeches, his red cotton shirt and decided to risk the dampness. Leaving the field, He headed into the nearest big town. He knew that Athens itself would take most of the day to walk. While he was walking, he noticed the remnants of a parade, bits of bunting, tiny pennant flags and ribbons, and one name stood out, screamed at you! Justinian's ultimate boss. The youth almost jumped for joy. But getting close to face the commander was a big problem. Once the commander focused on something, it was very hard to get his attention. Undeterred, Justinian looked for the nearest Roman garrison, which he found just after high noon. He approached the front building, the entrance way to the area of tents. He stood at attention and faced the front entrance guard. Justinian gave off a snappy salute and announced: Justinian Cornelius, Optio, legion IV. I would like to see the officer in charge.' The guard looked him over, 'Where is the rest of your uniform, soldier?'

'Sir, if you don't mind.'

'Sir, then, where is…'

'My cohort and some officers have been in captivity for several days. We're being held for ransom by some mutineers from the IV legion near the Greek island of Chios. My officer-in-charge, Agrippa helped me escape by boat yesterday morning. I've just managed to jump over board after hiding for two days. Here, feel,' Justinian offered the guard one of his loose garments, still soaking wet. The guard visibly relaxed and grabbed the garment 'Agrippa, you say?' he asked.

'Someone mention Agrippa?' and out strode Pompey, looking every inch the general, resplendent in his showy white armour and cloak. 'Young man, don't I know you?'

'Yes, general, and gave his best salute,' I'm Optio Justinian Cornelia, of the IVth legion, under the supervision of Prefect Agrippa.'

'Right, where's your supervisor. And, why are you half-dressed?'

Justinian, wearied, began to explain his circumstances and the situation back on the island. Pompey's jaw dropped. 'You mean we have pirates back again, after I cleaned them out?'

'Sir, these pirates are mutineers from the IVth legion auxiliaries.'

Orders began flying to and fro. Soldiers were sent to take control of the captive boat. Two further boats were seconded, filled with soldiers, and sent to the small island west of Chios. Still, nobody knew the name of the island. Pompey arranged his own boat and ordered Justinian to escort him to the mutineers. He also got twelve soldiers to accompany himself and the Optio. Just after mid-afternoon, the flotilla left Pireaus Harbour.

Chapter 21

That same evening, Agrippa tried to relax. The food supply was running out. Mutineers, as well as captives, were suffering from hunger pangs, feeling lethargic and beginning to get on each other's nerves. Their boat had been missing for three days. Agrippa worried about Justinian. Some response should have been made. The night was quiet, apart from some owls on their night rounds and, the waves made a steady crash on the shore. Agrippa lay on his back and studied the stars, so many and so far away. Sailors, he knew, used them to get from one location to another, fascinating. There were different constellations, different patterns. If there were cloud cover, they used magnets to guide them to their destinations. While Agrippa was pondering along these lines, a tribune officer joined him, sitting down next to him. 'I believe you are Agrippa the prefect of the IVth,' he said.

Agrippa nodded, 'Yes, correct. Who are you?'

'I'm Junius Septimus, a tribune of the soldiers.'

'Aah, yes, I've heard of you. Pleased to meet you,' and Agrippa extended his hand. They shook. 'You know, Agrippa, if we wanted to overcome these mutineers, now would be the time to do it.'

'Yes, I've given that some thought myself.'

‘The only problem, they’ve got weapons, we haven’t.’

‘That’s a huge problem…’ Agrippa started an answer.

‘There are weapons on the other side of the island.’

‘What!’

‘There’s a cave-temple with two priest-guards and they have knives. They don’t like pirates,’ Septimus informed the prefect.’

‘Who does the temple serve?’

‘Lost or wayward sea-men.’

‘That is fitting,’ Agrippa had to say, and then added, ‘Come on, let’s visit this temple for lost souls.’

As the prefect and the tribune made their way across the island, a group of thirty men were trudging their way along the shoreline towards the area where most of the mutineers were gathered. Their rate of progress was a little slow owing to the arthritic knees of the group’s senior leader. Justinian walked with them, rendering assistance whenever it was needed. Sometimes, the Magnus faltered, walking in the sand. Often, he held his head up high and swore; the Magnus hated pirates. He had fought against them for five years, eliminating the majority.

As they got nearer to the mutineer’s area, Justinian began to feel panic settling in. He was about to go into action once again with his trusty short sword. Men were going to be severely wounded, bloody death would ensue.

‘Pompey’s group were closing in on the slumbering mutineers, even the designated guard found it difficult to keep his eyes open. A sudden, blood-curdling scream erupted as two figures began threshing their way through the sleeping mutineers. Swords swapped hands, mutineers rose from their slumber only to be knocked down again, moaning, with nasty dagger gashes on their bodies. The Magnus gave the order for his soldiers to join the melee, and before long, the mutineers were grovelling for mercy.

Thirty-six mutineers were destined for crucifixion, this being the approved punishment for piracy. Included in the death squad were the two hired hands who raped Sabina. In a way, justice had turned full circle. The sentenced men remained on the island, as Agrippa and Justinian set sail for Athens, on their way home to Rome. The voyage home was uneventful, a full report of the mutinous events, was delivered to the senate. Three soldiers were mentioned in dispatches for bravery: Agrippa, prefect, IVth legion; Junius Septimus, tribune of the Soldiers, IVth legion, Justinian Cornelius, Optio, IVth legion. Each man is personally thanked by General Gneus, Pompey Magnus, before disembarking.

Chapter 22

'What are you reading at the moment, Antonia?'

'Some of Solon's writings, Greek political stuff is all,' she replied, not looking up from her parchment.

Justinian scratched his head, 'Where do you get all this archaic stuff from?'

She looked up to him, 'Uh, the library near the forum…' hesitating, she smiled at him, 'You're teasing me, yes?'

'Sister, I'm not really. I've been to Greece and I know all about the country and her history.' he declared in a lofty tone.

'Where was Solon born, then?'

'Somewhere in Greece, I expect.'

'Smarty! I don't know either. When I find out, I'll let you know.'

Justinian looked at his sister with a serious expression. 'Antonia, when we, ah, last got together, um'

'Justinian, I've got to tell you something, you might get upset over…'

'What?' his jaw dropped,

'You're not my real brother; you were adopted because mother thought she couldn't have children. After you were adopted, Julia came along, then me.'

'Jupiter!'

'Childless couples could easily adopt then, it's harder now.

'Antonia,' Justinian whispered, 'are you being serious?'

'Oh, Justinian, I'm so sorry. Now you understand how mother reacts the way she does. She's so filled with hurt; she cannot face you. She wanted to tell you the truth.'

'Oh, Jupiter!'

'Look, why don't you come with me, follow me, Justinian.' Antonia rose from her seat, took his hand, tugged him out of his seat and coaxed him into her bed chamber. Once inside the doorway, Antonia wrapped herself around Justinian. 'Oh, I've missed you so much, kiss me, please…'All thoughts, problems, cares suddenly became non-existent as Justinian held Antonia tightly. As he was off base, in the city, he was only wearing his military tunic and an under-garment. Antonia was dressed in a skimpy shawl, no under casts. Both were frantically pulling at each other's clothing to get it off. Justinian ceased, 'What about Julia?' he asked sheepishly. 'She's out with a new boyfriend, won't be home for ages,' replied Antonia, almost naked.

They spent most of the afternoon together, relaxing in the afterglow of coitus. Justinian though, became depressingly curious. 'Why didn't anyone tell me about my adoption? Who are my real parents?'

'Well, I didn't know. I was too young to understand,' she answered, her head resting in her hand, the crook of her elbow indenting the mattress. 'I don't think Julia knew until about three years ago.'

Antonia added, 'As for your real parents, he was an army officer, and they already had three sons.'

'You'll have to give me names, Antonia.'

‘He was a close friend of father’s; mother knows his name.’ With that, Antonia shuffled her body closer to his and attempted to get his flaccid penis ramrod hard. It was fruitless; Justinian’s mind was actively going through the implications of adoption.

Final Chapter

It was a balmy night when most folks stayed indoors and had a slave fan them. Those who couldn't afford a slave, had a younger member of the family fan them. Four men, walking through the dark Subura streets of Rome, looked very suspicious. All four of the men were wearing the same long white dress-coat; keeping off the main thoroughfare, the four men stopped outside a tavern and started having a discussion among themselves. One man stood out and, gave directions to the other three. It was difficult to identify these men.

They entered the tavern and looked into the dark recesses, where candles only served to identify persons who wish to remain unidentified, the four men walked from nook to nook and peered into the darkness. After the third recess, they stood still. The person they were looking for was staring at them. He had company, a woman was snuggled-up to him, and she was scantily dressed. 'Why don't you tell your girlfriend to go for a walk?' The tallest of the four men offered. Surrounded by darkness the figure tensed, 'Do not, I repeat, do not touch your dagger,' he ordered, adding, 'there are four short swords at the ready to slice you up.'

A growl, 'Right, right, what are you after?'

‘We want to question you about the arson attack on a young soldier’s house.’

The man tensed again, this time his tone was entirely different, ‘I dunno nothing about that. There are more short swords around now, lads.’

The four faceless men looked around to see they’d been joined by four more men who came out of the shadowy recesses. Their swords were in their hands.

A command was given, the four-man group erupted, the individuals each taking a different position to suddenly check each of the gang members. The two sets of swordsmen hurtled into each other, metal began flying and striking metal, the sound was unbearable, clash, clash, clash, one of the Subura gang members ended up on the floor, a neat gash on his upper arm. The odds were better now for the four visitors, but the knife man had disappeared. Another gang member fell hard on the floor, bleeding from an upper leg wound. The last two gang members slowly retreated as the Roman swords began to threaten them. Then, suddenly, the place was deserted. The gang members had made a run for it.

‘Have we lost the knife man?’ one soldier asked.

‘No, I’ve got two more men out there, they should be here soon.’

No sooner said, the two soldiers returned with this writhing body between them. ‘Here, you can have him,’ one of them said, and promptly pushed the hapless gang leader to the four Roman soldiers.

The knife man was checked for more weapons, none, and thrown into a chair, then hastily tied-up. ‘What do you want from me?’ he screamed.

‘Just shut it and we’ll tell you, you cretin,’ the lead soldier shouted.

‘About two months ago you took on a job to torch a house, a young soldier’s house, the son of a soldier who just died in Spain, as it happens, and we look after our comrades. He and his family have no home. What are you going to do about it?’

‘I know the house you are talking about, but I got the order from Crassus via Catalina. I was told that the residents were defaulting on their payments and had done so for six months, Crassus wanted it torched. The cost of rebuilding was nothing to him.’

‘So, the order came down via Catalina? You’ve been duped, my friend.’

‘You’d better talk to Catalina, then.’

‘No!’ The senior soldier yelled, that villa is going to be rebuilt and you, Catalina, Marcus Crassus and that scum, Geordanius are going to pay for the rebuilding costs.’

Two days later, Catalina was seen hobbling around the Subura streets with a crutch. A new villa was being built, paid for by a small band of fools. Geordanius had been found guilty of malicious killing of the young girl named Sabina and was declared *“nefas”,* therefore sentenced to twenty years exile.

Geordanius’s property was confiscated and handed over to Sabina’s mother. The dictator Sulla sanctioned the property transfer.